MW01119436

ROCK STARS

Team Gushue's Road to Gold

ROCK STARS

Team Gushue's Road to Gold

Robin Short

Foreword: Roy MacGregor

St. John's
Newfoundland and Labrador
2006

We gratefully acknowledge the financial support of The Canada Council for the Arts, the Government of Canada through the Book Publishing Industry Development Program (BPIDP), and the Government of Newfoundland and Labrador through the Department of Tourism, Culture and Recreation for our publishing program.

Design: Sarah Hansen

Published by
Creative Publishers
an imprint of CREATIVE BOOK PUBLISHING
a Transcontinental Inc. associated company
P.O. Box 1815, Station C.
St. John's, Newfoundland A1C 5P9

Printed in Canada by:
Transcontinental Inc.

National Library of Canada Cataloguing in Publication

Short, Robin, 1965-
Rock stars! : Team Gushue's road to gold / Robin Short ; foreword by Roy MacGregor.

ISBN 1-897174-12-8

1. Gushue, Brad. 2. Curling--Newfoundland and Labrador--Biography.
3. Curling--Canada--Biography. 4. Olympic Winter Games (20th : 2006 : Turin, Italy).
I. Title.

GV845.6.S58 2006   796.964092'2718   C2006-904164-4

FOREWORD

In early February of 2006, I headed for Italy and the Turin Olympics thinking that so much of it was entirely predictable. Canada would shine, as we always seem to shine in the Winter Games. Canada would panic early on, as always seems to be the case, but by the end all would be as it should be: gold medals in men's and women's hockey, stunning performances by the speedskaters, the usual figure skating controversy, and possibly even the odd surprise.

The Globe and Mail's Christie Blatchford and I flew over together from Toronto, me having first flown into Toronto from my home in Kanata, on the outskirts of Ottawa. We caught a Lufthansa flight that would put down in Frankfurt, where we would switch to another Lufthansa flight for Turin. We were barely over the Atlantic when the unexpected began. First the oxygen ran so thin that three people passed out and had to be laid out along the floor while they called, vainly, over the intercom for a doctor. Then, with the air back to normal and the plane landed safely in Frankfurt, they lost our luggage. And finally, about a storey and a half over the runway in Turin, the pilot suddenly, and dramatically, aborted his landing when a small plane wheeled out onto the runway.

It was certain to be an Olympics with stories.

I would never have guessed the most moving moment of these Games. The men's curling team – a gang of Newfoundlanders with a middle-aged ringer – somehow took the gold medal, and Christie wanted to head down to the Medals Plaza at Piazza Castella for the ceremony. I had anticipated being there with the men's hockey team, but this, remember, was the Olympics where very little took place as expected.

We arrived early, claiming good seats, and welcoming the free blankets the volunteers were handing out on such a cold, crisp night. At one point the air filled with tiny snowflakes, but soon it cleared off and the sky darkened and it was time for the presentation. We sat and watched, then stood and sang along as "O Canada" was played, and that crazy red-and-white flag we tend to ignore at home and wrap ourselves in abroad was raised up the pole. It was a chilling moment, with the weather having nothing to do with it.

I had not been to the curling venue and had never seen these athletes before. There were five of them, all dressed in their Hudson's Bay Company gear and now wearing huge, glittering Olympic gold medals around their necks. Knowing there had to be a story in this, we raced off to the side where there were stock-pens erected to separate the athletes from the media, and we took up our positions and waited. It looked ludicrous. The stock-pens and their maze were built to handle and control hundreds of journalists. There were maybe five of us, perhaps fewer. Christie and I on one side, a big hulking fellow in a large red jacket around the turn.

The curlers came down a ramp and onto the pavement and were then herded through the gates to the holding area, while the Medals Plaza turned its attention to the next set of victors.

I did not then know who they were, although obviously they were friendly and, as expected, marvelously quotable. One of them – later identified as Mike Adam, the fifth member and the one who usually watched from the sidelines – came alongside me, plucked up his medal and said, in that wonderful accent that tickles all the way to the punchline: "Jeez, if they'd only put a magnet on the back of her, I could put it on my fridge, eh?"

This was going to be a great story – only, only, only…they weren't stopping for us, the all-important *national* media. They were heading for the big guy around the corner. They were heading for Robin Short's notebook.

Christie and I and the other *Globe* reporters stationed in the city for the Games – Gary Mason, Dave Naylor, Bev Smith – got to know Robin over those three weeks. We stayed in a university residence far from the Medals Plaza in a charming little village called Grugliasco where, in the evenings after we had filed our stories, we would file again, out into the streets in search of pasta and red wine. It was a small Canadian contingent, and Robin instantly became a key part of it.

We liked his humour. We liked his insights. We marveled at the knowledge he had of curling and of this specific team. All of us have known journalists who "own" a beat – some of us pride ourselves in being pretty good in certain areas ourselves, Christie in the courts, Gary on The West, Dave on the Canadian Football League – but all were in awe of Robin Short's command and ownership of curling. He not only knew all the out-turns of the game, he knew, and understood, all the in-turns of this complicated team that had accomplished so much when so little was expected.

That he would write a book about this remarkable victory is only right. Only he could do it. And besides, he, too, is part of that story whether he realizes it or not.

On the button, Robin. On the button.

Roy MacGregor
July, 2006

INTRODUCTION

They stared into the clear Italian night, each athlete decked out in crimson and white, and their attire highlighted by the marvelous 600-gram jewelry dangling from their necks. The CD-sized Olympic gold medal (it's actually made of silver but coated with six grams of gold) twinkled in the lights of the Medals Plaza. On their heads and feet they wore those goofy-looking, fur-lined, ear-flap hats and mukluks, the kind that trappers need for the Labrador wilderness. Yet, dammit, didn't they look good, standing as one, with the Canadian anthem filling the night air?

They were deep in Turin's inner city, and just "draw weight" in curling vernacular from Via Roma where the beautiful people stroll on marble tiles, window-shopping for fashions by trendy Versace, Armani, Gucci, and Fendi. Medals Plaza is in the heart of Piazza Castella, a town square that is a familiar sight in Italy. Surrounding Piazza Castella you can see breathtaking architecture dating back centuries. Close by is Cattedrale di San Giovanni Battista (il Duomo), which houses Cappella della Sacra Sindone, or Chapel of the Holy Shroud. It is dedicated to the relic believed by many to be the burial cloth in which Jesus was wrapped. This Shroud is no longer kept in the chapel and is only exhibited for public showing every twenty years.

The five Canadian curlers had bagged their big prize amongst these sights in Italy at the 20th Winter Games. Olympic gold for Brad Gushue,

Mark Nichols, Russ Howard, Jamie Korab, and fifth man Mike Adam. Kevin Martin, a 2002 Olympic silver medalist and still among Canada's curling elite, couldn't do it. Neither could Mike Harris, the 1998 Olympic runner-up. Jeff Stoughton and Randy Ferbey, both Brier and world champions, took their best shot at the Olympic Trials just over two months prior to the Olympics. So did John Morris, who, until he joined forces with Martin in the spring of 2006 was on the cusp of skipping a Brier championship team. They all whiffed. The men's hockey team, which arrived in Italy facing even greater pressure than the Canadian women's hockey squad, drew great big pizza pies: back-to-back shutout losses to Switzerland and Finland. When it was over, the 2002 gold medalists in hockey from the Salt Lake City Games sat fourth; Brodeur, Iginla, Pronger, and Sakic had been sent to the sidelines.

With the men's hockey team plummeting down the Italian Alps, who could we rally around? The women's hockey team? Certainly, but with Sweden upsetting the Americans in the semifinal, the only way Canada could lose was by showing up in joggers rather than Bauers. It was no surprise when Canada won 4-1 in the final. There was also Cindy Klassen, the Winnipegger who would become Canada's darling of Turin with five medals. Klassen's gold, two silver, and a pair of bronze were two more than any Canadian athlete had ever won at an Olympic Games. Remarkable indeed, but this was speed skating, and not everyone understands this combination of sprinting, endurance, and occasional aggression.

Curling was another matter altogether. The Americans, despite Pete Fenson's success in Turin, don't seem to know an inturn from an outturn, although this Wisconsin pizza man is quickly emerging as one of the world's elite curlers. Meanwhile, in Italy, where the official curling registration is said to hover around 500 but in reality is in the 150 range, a young rocker wannabe was thrilling audiences in Pinerolo, the "second Olympic city", just outside Turin and where the curling events were staged.

Brad Gushue's coach, Jeff Thomas, tries to cheer up the young curler after he arrives home from the 2000 Canadian junior championship. Gushue's expression says it all. *(Don Power/The Express photo)*

With his tight curling pants and Prada designer eyewear, Joel Retornaz brought pizzazz if nothing else to the ice. Locals filled the arena's seats and school children shrieked "EEE-tal-ia! EEE-tal-ia!" on each Italian shot. Never in the history of the game would there be louder applause for such nondescript, routine takeouts. Retornaz would peter out with a pair of losses to close out the round-robin, but not before causing a stir in the curling world with a 4-5 record. This ranked them higher than 3-6 Sweden skipped by Peja Lindholm, a three-time world champ who had been one of the pre-tourney favourites. Canada was expected to do well, and curling fans knew this was a special team, even if it didn't look that way from the onset.

At Medals Plaza, close to 1,000 ticket holders gathered for the curling presentation. Among the group of onlookers was Canada's coach, Toby McDonald, whose controlled guidance helped steer the ship through rocky waters. (In the Olympics, unfortunately, coaches are not awarded gold medals.) Outside the gated Plaza, thousands more filled neighbouring streets, including Via Garibaldi, the popular outdoor pedestrian mall where shops and cafes line the cobblestone streets. But it wasn't the men's and women's curling champions the throng had come to see. It was Ricardo Cocciante. Italy's famous singer was headlining one of a series of post-medal concerts throughout the Games, joining the likes of aging rocker Lou Reed, pop diva Whitney Houston, and America Idol Kelly Clarkson.

On the stage, however, Brad Gushue was oblivious to the scene around him. He was poised where only a select few in the world would ever stand. And when the first strain of "O Canada" was played, he appeared to choke back a tear. Later, he mouthed the words, "I love you, Mom" to the final chord of the anthem.

There was no holding back the tears in 2000 in Moncton, New Brunswick, at the Canadian Junior Curling Championship. Just nineteen years old at the time, Gushue settled into the hack, the rubber footrests from where curlers deliver their shot, and stared down the 140 feet of pebbled ice that is a curling surface, a distance that separated him from his first national championship. It was overtime at the Karcher Canadian final and Gushue owned last shot, an easy draw to the rings, the two painted circles at each end of the ice that forms the house, or scoring area. How many times had the young man from Newfoundland made that shot? Hundreds? Thousands, maybe?

Gushue took a deep breath and launched into his delivery. The shot, he would say later, felt good coming out of his hands. But sweepers Jamie Korab and Mike Adam knew different. They went to work quickly, soon supported by Mark Nichols, who was calling line – keeping an eye to the path of the shot. Gushue looked on with a combination of worry, surprise, and then terror. Confronting the inevitable, he turned and looked away, his trip to Europe sliding away with the wayward stone. The shot would come up short of the house, giving British Columbia's Brad Kuhn a steal of one in the extra end and an 8-7 win. With the national championship came a berth in the 2000 World Junior Championship in Germany. Gushue managed to contain himself, at least through the television interviews and until the lights went down. And that's when he broke down.

Brad Kuhn of British Columbia tries to console Brad Gushue after the Canadian junior championship in 2000.

(Canadian Press photo)

Looking on was Russ Howard, who had moved to Moncton in 1997 from his native Ontario. In Canada, he was "Mr. Curling," a Hall of Famer with a pair of Brier and World Championship victories, and the record-holder for most wins at the National Men's Championship. Howard was the reason Gushue started curling at thirteen back at the St. John's Curling Club in Newfoundland. He was in the stands that Sunday afternoon in February, 2000, watching the junior final. After the game, Howard noticed the Newfoundland skip fighting desperately – but with little success – to hold back tears.

Howard went up to Gushue to console him. "Don't worry," the legend said. "Shit happens. It's the nature of the game. You'll get over it." It was little consolation to Gushue, suffering from a broken heart on the eve of Valentine's Day.

Nobody could have predicted that six years later he and Gushue, Nichols, Korab and Adam (the latter whose starting job Howard would seize) might combine to deliver Canada its first Olympic Men's Curling gold medal.

CHAPTER 1

Those who know Brad Gushue probably aren't surprised that he has enjoyed the pinnacle of curling triumph at an early age. Brier or no Brier, it does not get any bigger than the Olympic stage. When you spend even a bit of time with Gushue, you soon understand what makes him tick and why he would aim for those heights. If asked about his attributes, he can count them on one hand. He describes himself as driven, focused, and demanding – but not necessarily in that order. Others may consider him a bit arrogant, although what successful athlete does not have a bit of an edge to their personality?

Brad Gushue describes himself as "driven, focused and demanding."

(Joe Gibbons/The Telegram photo)

In his high school yearbook, Gushue lists "competing in the Olympics" as his goal. If there was ever a thought of chucking aside the broom after that heart-wrenching loss in Moncton, it was only for a fleeting moment. Instead, recalls Reg Caughie, then manager of Gushue's home rink at the St. John's Curling Club, the youngster was quickly back on the ice when he flew home to Newfoundland. "He stayed away from the club for a while," said Caughie, whose alter ego has been Brier Bear (the Brier's furry mascot) at the past twenty-six Canadian Men's Curling Championships. "I didn't see him for a week, I suppose. But he called one day and asked if there was any ice available. I said, 'Yes, my son, come on down.' He threw forty-eight rocks and every one of them was in the house. He came off the ice and said, 'I'm back. I'm ready.'"

> "… quitting was about the worst thing you could do, almost a cowardly thing. The best way to come back from a loss was to win the next year. It made me driven. It was the turning point in my career."
>
> - BRAD GUSHUE

"I never really thought of quitting," Gushue explains. "I was real disappointed, sure, did the whole sooky eighteen- or nineteen-year-old thing. But once I smartened up, I realized there was only one way to go, and quitting was about the worst thing you could do, almost a cowardly thing. The best way to come back from a loss was to win the next year. It made me driven. It was the turning point in my career."

In curling, as in any sport, a little luck goes a long way. In 2000, the Canadian Curling Association opted to raise the age limit for junior curlers from "nineteen and under" to "twenty and under" beginning with the next curling season. The move gave Gushue and Nichols, both twenty years old, a reprieve. Nichols, in fact, still only squeezed in by twenty-four hours because he turned twenty-one on New Years Day, just under the age requirement deadline. Adam, at nineteen, was safe, but the twenty-one-year-old Korab was not eligible. He was replaced by eighteen-year-old Brent Hamilton, who would throw second stone and curl a perfect 100 % in the national final. But Gushue was not entirely focused on making what would be a record sixth appearance at the junior nationals. He had bigger things in mind. He wanted a berth in the Brier.

Gushue, Nichols, Adam, and coach Jeff Thomas met over coffee at a Tim Hortons outlet, where the skip had to be persuaded to play out his final junior year. Nichols and Adam wanted another crack at the nationals. So did Thomas, and Gushue said his parents encouraged him to play junior. "I decided there was only one way the year could be a success in junior and that was to win the world championship. Anything else was a failure," said Gushue, who was admittedly intrigued at the thought of jumping to men's competition.

CURLING TERMS

HACKS

Rubber grips in the ice used during the delivery.

"Looking back at it now," Thomas says, "we're sitting in a Tim Hortons, people around us are drinking coffee and eating donuts and we're talking about winning a world curling championship, that nothing else is acceptable. It's really something when you think about it." Hamilton was brought aboard, and Gushue made it clear what the playing rules were: either we win the worlds or nothing at all.

It had been twenty-four years since Newfoundland had celebrated any kind of meaningful curling championship. In 1976, Jack MacDuff, Toby McDonald, Doug Hudson, and Ken Templeton won Newfoundland's first and only Brier. MacDuff had been an air traffic controller stationed in St. John's, but he had long since moved out of the province. He settled in Moncton and, like Russ Howard, watched as Gushue coughed up that last shot in the 2000 final. But MacDuff liked what he saw in the determined skip the next year. Templeton was even more effusive. "I truly believe he's destined for bigger things," he said of Gushue. Not bad for a kid who threw his first inturn at what might be considered the ripe old age of thirteen.

Gushue, like thousands of other Canadian youngsters, was a hockey player. As TSN devoted more and more TV time to the "Roaring Game" (named for the sound of rocks traveling over the pebbled ice), however, Gushue took notice. His favourite would soon become "ol' Hurry Hard," the leather-lunged Howard. Intrigued with a game that integrated brains and skill, Gushue decided to finally try it. "My last game of hockey was the day before my first game of curling. I went home and told Mom 'I'm not playing hockey anymore.' She said, 'Well, you're going to have to tell your father.' I didn't want to tell Dad because I knew he'd be pissed off. But I told him, said I liked curling. And he had just spent five or six hundred dollars on equipment. He fired the bag down the basement stairs and went back to work."

Brad Gushue delivers his shots right-handed even though he's a left-hander. *(Joe Gibbons/The Telegram photo)*

The game and those who are attracted to it, as Howard can attest, has undergone extraordinary change over the years. Gone are the days when it appealed almost exclusively to the social elite. It's enjoyed by all classes, from the taxi drivers and other blue-collar workers who reveled in Gushue's gold, to the white-collar staff who control Newfoundland's offshore oil. But when Gushue ventured through the doors of the St. John's Curling Club in early winter of 1993, the game still had an uppity way to it. However, Gushue liked its appeal. Curling is about precision and finesse and matching intellect with your opponent. He had played chess as a youngster and loved the whole mental process that came with curling: thinking two or three or even four moves ahead of your opponent. It had an athleticism to it, too. "And there was a smaller team. I really like individual sports, and while curling's a team sport, it's very individual as well. I love that balance."

The team rolled through the 2001 provincial junior championship unbeaten, telling the St. John's *Telegram* afterwards it was but the first step in the team's ultimate goal – a world junior championship. It was the first public admission of their thirst for the ultimate goal in curling.

It was also an example of Gushue's drive and ambition. In fact, he has often been described as twenty-five going on fifty, an old man in young man's skin. Some will say he's almost too straight-laced. Clean-cut with a wholesome image, Gushue knows when to say all the right things. He is as articulate as he is astute. It's perhaps why he was picked at age thirteen to film a school milk ad for television. Even today, Gushue rarely drinks. He will indulge a couple of beers, perhaps two or three times a year and on special occasions. Otherwise, his regular drink is root beer.

Away from the ice, says Nichols, Gushue will often let his hair down. On the road, he'll joke around as much as the next guy in the hotel room, although he's "more serious," Nichols adds. "But he's just like the rest of us, if you know what I mean. He's partied, had a lot of fun. Everyone grows out of it at different times, and he kind of got sick of it before the rest of us did." Away from the rink, Gushue may be somewhat of a house cat. He'll watch movies or sports (he lists the Blue Jays, Maple Leafs, and Vijay Singh as his favourites), or flick on a CD from a varied collection that includes everything from Garth Brooks to Eminem. He's actually left-handed, though he delivers a rock with his right hand and he may even pick on a guitar, although he knows only one song – "Drunken Sailor." On the ice, however, he's far from relaxed, says Nichols. "He's very focused and very serious, and that's what gets him through, I suppose. Everyone is different. Some people can't perform when they're too stressed or too focused."

"If Jamie isn't having fun, there's no point in him being out there. I'm a type A personality," Gushue says. "My mind is always working. It would be nice for one day to shut it all off, but I'm always thinking, always worrying about the positives and negatives of things."

Emotions can sometimes get the better of Brad Gushue. He has been known to bang a broom or even give it a fling after a bad end. If he was a hockey player, Gushue would be a player you would pound to get him off his game. To prepare for the 2001 junior nationals in St. Catharines, Ontario, and ultimately the worlds in Ogden, Utah, the Gushue team was looking to control their emotions, and to get an extra edge. They found the answers by building strength both physically and mentally. In addition to working out, the curlers began seeing sports psychologist Dr. Basil (Bas) Kavanagh at Memorial University in St. John's.

Gushue would later give as much credit to Kavanagh for the world junior and Olympic gold medals as he would to anyone else. "I thought I knew everybody in sport," says Kavanagh, a former Memorial varsity basketball coach and current provincial hoops president. "I agreed to meet with Brad. I just didn't know who he was. I didn't know anything about curling, and when I sat there, it was absolutely incredulous that this twenty-year-old kid would say to me, 'I want to win [junior] provincials, I want to win the Canadian [junior] title. I want to win the worlds. I want to go to the Brier, I want to qualify for the Olympic Trials, and I want to go to the Olympics.'

"I was actually looking at him, and although I'm sure my face didn't show any reaction or emotion, I was laughing inside," Kavanagh told the St. John's *Express*. "I was saying, 'Who is this guy!?!' But Gushue wasn't laughing." Gushue was dead serious, and he expected the same of the other curlers. He can be very demanding, admitting he is probably not the easiest curler in the world with whom you could play.

While he does not expect anybody to put the same amount of time and effort into the game as he does, "I do expect them to put in a certain level of work. If they reach that level, I am very easy to deal with, very easy to play with. If they don't reach that level or put in the effort, I can be their worst nightmare," he says with the hint of a smile. "There have been teammates who have not put in the effort, and you cannot get results if you don't put in the effort. If I am putting in as much time as I do, and I see somebody who is not competing or training as hard, I get a little upset."

A scratch golfer, and one of Newfoundland and Labrador's best before he cut back his links time to concentrate on off-season training for curling, Gushue says he would often head to the driving range or putting green before or after a tournament round. Meanwhile, the other golfers would lead a charge to the nearest watering hole. In his way of thinking, if you are going to do something, why not go full bore at 100%?

The St. John's team arrived in southern Ontario for the 2001 Canadian Junior's supremely confident, soaring through the round-robin at 9-3. Along the way, Gushue shattered John Morris's record of thirty-three wins as a skip at the nationals. It was the Morris team that added Gushue as a fifth man for the 1998 world championship which Canada won, the first of two straight world crowns for Morris. The

Newfoundland and Labrador foursome earned a bye to the final in St. Catharines after beating both Northern Ontario and Manitoba, both of whom were also 9-3, in the round-robin. As the latter two rinks battled it out in the semifinal, Gushue and his team stayed busy bowling.

When asked on the eve of the championship game if he would be in the same situation as the year previous in Moncton, with last shot for the win in an extra end, Gushue's reply was simple: "I won't miss." And there would be no need to worry. This time under the television lights, instead of wilting, the Gushue team shone, dismantling Mike McEwen's squad from Manitoba 8-3. It was Newfoundland and Labrador's first Canadian Junior Curling Championship. Just what Gushue had envisioned. "I was never one to doubt myself, but after what happened in Moncton and what some people were saying and others probably thinking, I suppose a few doubts crept into my mind. But I tried to convince myself I could do it. I never lost complete belief in myself. This is a reward for Moncton, I guess."

The ghost of 2000 had been exorcised. But the best was yet to come. ♠

CHAPTER 2

There have been a few faces come and go with Gushue curling teams over the years, but the one constant through it all – from the Moncton failure, through the 2001 world juniors and ultimately the Olympics – has been the sure-handed, heavy-hitting Mark Nichols at third (the third, or vice-skip, throws his/her two rocks just before the skip). Nichols, like Mike Adam, is from Labrador City. While Gushue, Adam, and Jamie Korab all dabbled in hockey as youngsters before finding their calling on curling ice, Nichols was a curler from the outset. He has the photos to prove it, including one showing a two-year-old blonde boy on curling ice propped up by his parents. (Not that he didn't skate. His father would construct a backyard rink every winter – in the perfect Labrador elements – and upwards of a dozen neighbourhood kids would skate there every evening.)

> **"We could not have done what we've done without Mark Nichols throwing third stone."**
> - BRAD GUSHUE

For young Mark and his sister Shelley, who curled in the 2006 national Scott Tournament of Hearts, curling would be their obvious calling. After all, their mother played in the nationals with the great Sue Anne Bartlett, Newfoundland's all-time winningest female skip and a

Canadian curling Hall of Famer. And their father was a pretty fine curler, too. Nichols was introduced to curling as a seven-year-old in Grade two and had just turned twelve when he curled in his first provincial junior championship as lead.

If Gushue is the intense one of the lot, and Adam and Korab the buoyant personalities, Nichols is the quiet one. His game, however, creates plenty of noise. The special relationship between Gushue and Nichols began eight years ago when the two hooked up in the provincial junior final. Like many athletes from Labrador, Nichols landed on the island portion of the province a relative unknown – except to Gushue. The shy newcomer was, in Gushue's estimation, better than any player he had on his St. John's team. And so he thought, 'Why am I knocking heads with this guy when we should be playing together and competing on the national level?' Nichols was a high school senior and had intended to attend university on the mainland, likely Waterloo, Ontario, to study computer science. But Gushue got talking to Nichols and eventually convinced him to attend Memorial University in St. John's and curl third for him.

The 2001 World Junior Championship was held in Ogden, Utah, just north of Salt Lake City. Despite losing his first game to the U.S., Gushue roared back with six straight wins. *(Canadian Press photo)*

Their first year curling together was 1999. They've been teammates ever since. "When I first moved here, he was the only guy I knew," says Nichols of Gushue. "He had a car and he'd pick me up from MUN. I hung around with him all the time until Mike moved down the next year. Then it was me, him, and Mike. We were three best buds."

Throughout the annals of sport, it's often been said that long-time teammates – especially the really good ones – come to know each other better than anyone, spouses included, in the rink or on the court or on the field. On the other ice, Howe and Abel thought and played as one. Same with Gretzky and Kurri. "Even though I was sweeping this year [Howard held the broom on last shot] and the last couple of years, Brad usually asked me what I thought in situations," says Nichols. "From the other end of the ice, most of the time I can tell what shot Brad will call before he actually calls it." For as good a shooter as Gushue is, in many corners Nichols is considered to be on par with his skip. In

The Gushue curling team, Brad Gushue says, could not have accomplished what it has without third stone Mark Nichols.

(Joe Gibbons/The Telegram photo)

fact, Gushue pointedly says today, "We could not have done what we've done without Mark Nichols throwing third stone."

Both Nichols and Gushue were voted to the first all-star team at the 2000 junior nationals, with Nichols following up with another all-star selection in 2001 after leading all thirds at eighty-one per cent. In the final game against Manitoba, Nichols curled ninety per cent. Brent Hamilton, the only high schooler on the team, shot the lights out against Manitoba, curling a perfect 100 %.

Jamie Korab was too old to play in the 2001 Canadian juniors, so the team added Brent Hamilton, right, who was still in high school at the time. *(Canadian Press photo)*

Gushue's game is taken from the curling textbook, technically strong with an ability to play a wide-open, aggressive game, although he can also engage in a defensive struggle when needed. He can throw heavy weight and make the delicate draws. Nichols' forte is the big hit, throwing big weight against a full house. His long raise double takeout (a removal of two opposing stones) in the sixth end against Finland in the Olympic gold-medal game was a shot for the ages. But long before that big hit in Italy, a knockout punch which set up the famous "Torino Six" (Gushue scored six in the sixth end) and sent the Finns to the canvas, Nichols was making big shots on the world stage.

At the 2001 World Junior final in Ogden, Utah, Canada and Denmark's Casper Bossen were tied 6-6 after nine ends with Gushue holding hammer. Both teams were down to their final four rocks and Bossen had a pair of well-placed centre line guards. On his first shot, Nichols made a perfect double and followed up with a peel of another Bossen guard, opening a path to the rings for Gushue. It was vintage Nichols, who received yet more all-star honours at the worlds. "At this level," Gushue had said, "Mark Nichols is among the world's elite."

Scenic Utah was an interesting setting for Nichols' performance. More than 150 years ago, Brigham Young led close to 5,000 disciples of the fledgling Mormon church across the United States, through the Great Plains and over the Rocky Mountains in search of a new home. The Church of Jesus Christ of Latter Day Saints settled in a land that was virgin Utah, on the shores of Great Salt Lake and in the shadows of the Canyonlands to the north. Nestled between the Wasatch National Forest and Great Salt Lake, Ogden was a picturesque, if nondescript, city. Its claim to fame? It provided the setting for the one-time television series "Touched by an Angel."

Ogden is in the heart of Mormon country, where the only sport that matters – outside of its world-renowned skiing in nearby Park City – is basketball. Utah boasts only one big-league team, the NBA's Utah Jazz, which plays in Salt Lake City, thirty minutes to the south. But the Jazz may be the state's fourth squad on the Fan Favourite Meter, behind Provo's Brigham Young University, the University of Utah, and Southern Utah. In 2001, all three colleges had reached the NCAA Tournament. Even Ogden's Weber State U – whose campus played host to the world juniors at the aptly-named Ice Sheet – offered an NCAA Division One basketball program.

Curling, to be sure, was not on the radar in these parts. Decked in their red and white Team Canada outfits, the curlers were asked on Ogden's streets if they were skiers, bobsledders, or snowboarders. Korab often recalls how one woman at Salt Lake City International Airport wondered

aloud if the world curling championship was a hairstyling competition.
But Ogden was pegged to play host to the 2001 junior worlds because the
Olympic Winter Games were slated for the next year in Salt Lake City.
(In curling, the world juniors are usually held in the selected Olympic site a
year before the Games. Saskatchewan's Kyle George, for example, won the
2005 world junior championship at the Pinerolo Palaghiaccio, where the
2006 Olympic curling competition would be played.)

Perhaps the Newfoundlanders and Labradorians felt somewhat at
home in Utah, with the state's Newfoundland Mountain Range not too
far off in the distance. But there was no mistaking who had the home-
ice advantage in the tournament opener. The United States, skipped by
Andy Roza from that curling hotbed of Omaha, Nebraska, doubled Team
Gushue 8-4. (Roza, by the way, would watch Gushue win Olympic gold
five years later. The American made the trip to Turin from Rome where
he was serving at the Vatican after joining the priesthood.)

As a group, Gushue and Co. curled only sixty-seven per cent against
the United States. "To curl in the sixties is not acceptable," Gushue said.
"We should be in the seventies." The Canadians were heavy on a lot of
their shots, very uncharacteristic of the Gushue team. Adam, curling
lead, particularly struggled with his weight, a trend that would continue
throughout the week. Nichols would later say the team gathered following
that opening-day loss for a tête-à-tête. They all agreed they had to smarten
up; simply lacing up their shoes wasn't enough to win a game against the
best juniors in the world. A red maple leaf did not guarantee victory. The
team would have another similar meeting five years later in Turin, Italy.

Watching Adam toss first rocks was Korab, the team's fifth. It would
be a reversal of roles in Turin as Adam was relegated to alternate, replaced
by Howard. Korab, at twenty-one, was too old to curl in the nationals, but
he met the age criteria for the worlds under the World Curling Federation
rules. When Gushue won the Canadian championship in St. Catharines,

Ontario, Korab was watching from Stephenville, Newfoundland, where he was competing for a St. John's men's team in the provincial championship.

Canada's poor outing in its first game was puzzling if only because it was likely no team in Ogden had arrived more prepared than Canada. "It's been a lot of work," Nichols had said, "more than I put into school ... harder than I've ever worked before."

"We hated going to school," added Gushue, "but we looked forward to practice. There hasn't been one day we considered it work." In fact, the St. John's Curling Club became the team's home away from home. When they weren't playing in the local Super League, the curlers were practicing. And practicing some more. "There were times," recalled Reg Caughie, the former curling club manager, "when it would be snowing pretty good outside and I'd be ready to close up when those boys would show up at the door. I'd say, 'Ah, come on in.' "

It wasn't unusual for the four to each toss as many as 200 rocks per day, four or five times a week. When their school schedules conflicted, they would practice on their own. When they managed to get together, they would often focus on playing a single shot, for upwards of two hours. "We're not going to improve much if we're just going to go out and mindlessly throw rocks," Gushue said. "We had sweepers on every rock in practice. We tried to put it as close to a game situation in our practices as we possibly could."

Call it jitters, or simply a case of missed shots, it didn't take Canada long to rebound from the loss to the United States. Gushue's team peeled off six straight wins to grab a share of top spot on the leader board with the Americans in Ogden. Despite the 6-1 record, though, there was still some cause for concern. The team's front end, Adam and Hamilton, were shaky, bailed out time and again by Nichols and Gushue. Adam, the personable lead, was particularly spotty. "I'm nowhere near acceptable standards," he said, refusing to dip into a bag of excuses. The front end's game, or lack thereof, was evident in the next-to-last round-robin game when Scotland registered a 9-6 win over Canada, eliminating any chance of a first-place finish.

While the Canadians were losing, the Americans were beating up on Denmark. The Scots were skipped by David Edwards of Lockerbie. His brother, Kenneth, played second. The team was lucky to get past the United States border and customs agents because of the foot-and-mouth outbreak that had devastated livestock in Great Britain. Lead Graham Sloan, who lived on a farm in Lockerbie, had to stay with friends during the days and weeks prior to the worlds to ensure his entry into America.

As for the Edwards boys, they were just plain lucky. On December 21, 1988, one of the world's worst air disasters occurred 35,000 feet above Lockerbie. Pan-Am Flight 103 was blown up by a terrorist's bomb and all 270 people aboard, and eleven on the ground, were killed. The Edwards family home was obliterated when part of the plane's wing plummeted onto it. Luckily, David and Kenneth were delivering Christmas gifts with their mother at the time. Their father, David, who was in the garage when the wing crashed down, barely escaped death.

Back in Ogden, Adam and Hamilton had trouble with their draw weight against the Scots, sending a number of rocks through the house. "Their front end was totally dominant of ours," fumed Gushue. "Mark and I were playing shots we shouldn't have to play at this level. At nationals, whenever Mike played over eighty per cent, we won. Same here. Whenever he curls eighty per cent, we win. But I think he's had one game over eighty per cent and that's not real good for us." Canada closed out the round-robin the next day with a win over France, finishing at 7-2. A semifinal rematch against Scotland was next. It wasn't even close. The Gushue team dominated, winning 7-1 in seven ends. "We sent a message," Nichols said.

Gushue also seemed to have sent a message to Adam, and the lead responded, dominating his Scottish counterpart, Sloan, eighty-nine per cent to sixty-one per cent in his best effort in Ogden. "It's like two curling rocks off my shoulders," Adam said. Only the Danes, who upset the Americans in the other semifinal, stood between Gushue and Newfoundland and Labrador's first real world championship in sporting circles. At the time, Ogden was also playing host to the world junior women's championship, and the Canadian girls were in the hunt for gold, too. Canada, skipped by Suzanne Gaudet of Prince Edward Island, was in the final against Sweden's Matilda Mattsson. With Gushue in the stands, Mattsson had only a simple draw to the rings for the win, but she lost when her final stone glided through the house giving the P.E.I. rink the win.

But Gushue didn't need to worry. Lightning would not strike twice. Thanks in part to Nichols' fine shot-making, and some skillful deliveries himself, Gushue beat Denmark's Bossen 7-6 the next day in the men's final, the winning point coming on a routine hit-and-stick on last shot. "I sat there and visualized the shot before I threw it," said Gushue. "When I let it go, I knew I made it because I threw it as good as I possibly could. Halfway down, it was going right on the nose. It was an amazing feeling watching it and knowing you've made the shot."

Said Toby McDonald, who at that time had been merely an interested observer of the team: "I hope this inspires everybody to greater things."

Little did he know he would be a part of that inspiration. ⬤

CHAPTER 3

While the world junior curling championship garners some attention in Canada, it's a non-entity in much of the sporting world, even in a curling country such as Scotland. In Canada, TSN televised the final on tape delay March 25. However, when Team Canada arrived home in St. John's a little more than twenty-four hours after the win over Denmark, the curlers were startled. They had a welcome that surpassed any homecoming a Canadian hockey team would receive if they were returning from a world junior championship.

In the early morning hours of March 27, St. John's International Airport was jammed with hundreds of supporters who burst into tumultuous applause when the curling team emerged into the arrivals area. Young and old came with homemade posters and banners, and some had tears in their eyes. Many of the fans knew the curlers. Many more didn't, but they wanted to be on hand for the historic moment. Who knew there would be another one for Gushue, Nichols, Korab, and Adam only five years later?

The team proudly displayed their awards and carried silver plates to commemorate their achievement. They had asked to bring the trophy home, but were refused by the World Curling Federation, which keeps the hardware. "We didn't do it for trophies or medals," Gushue explained to reporters. "It's just for the pride of being the best in Canada ... and the world. If we got nothing, we'd still be just as happy." Over the next couple of weeks, the team was lavished with honor after honor. The first was a parade through downtown St. John's. Later, Gushue and his teammates were given the "Freedom of the City" honour during a gala dinner at City Hall. Then their curling shoes were bronzed, and put on display at the St. John's Curling Club, next to the footwear the MacDuff team had worn in 1976.

Only two months after the Ogden win, Gushue started planning for the 2001-02 curling season. It would be his first year curling at the men's level, and despite having just emerged from the junior ranks, he was considered a favourite to win the provincial championship and represent Newfoundland at the Brier. These were certainly next on his list of things to do. In fact, Gushue taped a list of goals on the back of his bedroom door. They would be the last thing he saw before he flicked off the lights, and the first when he opened his eyes. The details were simple and concise: national junior championship, world junior title, provincial men's title, Brier championship, Olympic Trials, Olympic gold medal.

CURLING TERMS

RINGS

Concentric circles that together form the house.

This ambitious plan was undoubtedly the work of Kavanagh at Memorial University. Many top-flight curling teams were beginning to dabble in the use of sports psychology, including Nova Scotia's Colleen Jones, who had run off a string of four straight Canadian women's curling championships from 2001-04. "They had that same team [earlier] and weren't real successful and look at them," Gushue said to the Canadian

Press at the 2004 Brier in Saskatoon. "I think they are far superior mentally to other teams. We're trying to work on the [same] things that build confidence. Even if it's false confidence, it's better than no confidence."

And confidence, according to Kavanagh, is the key. So is focus. Curlers, after all, have to deliver a curling rock over 100 feet of changing ice, avoiding obstacles before coming to rest within centimeters of a target. Kavanagh instilled in the curlers a specific mindset: do not recall the missed shots, just look ahead to future games. He also developed what he called "imagery scripts." They were, quite simply, motivational tapes or CDs in their own voice that the players listened to periodically. For Gushue, it was every day, whether he was curling or taking an occasional off-day. There were also the reminders taped around the Gushue household, such as "I am the best at calling line," and "I believe I can become an Olympic champion."

Brad Gushue and Kevin Martin hooked up in the final of the Players Championship at Mile One Stadium in St. John's. Martin won in a game that would feature the 2002 Olympic silver medalist and eventual 2006 Olympic gold-medal champion.

(Don Power/The Express photo)

For the scripts, Gushue would detail his day at the Brier or another event from the point of waking up and showering, to riding in a van to the rink and listening to music barking from its speakers. He would feel the clothes he was slipping into, and sense his curling shoes sliding over his feet. He would hear the talk during the pre-game warm-up and describe how he felt

– calm, cool, and confident. He would hear the fans and the sound of the rock breaking over the pebble. And he would hear the unmistakable noise of granite crushing into granite.

There were mental images of strategy as well. He would go over all of his shots, especially the draws and takeouts. He would remind himself how good he felt when he did everything right. Then he would set up the game-winning shot, which, of course, he made. And then he would set the scene for the post-game celebration. Gushue and the others (each had their own imagery script) would listen to this training mantra constantly. On the day of the Olympic gold medal game, Gushue tuned in to his own voice: "Today is the day we have planned for. It is Canada's day, it is Newfoundland and Labrador's day. But most importantly, it is our day."

If you think this is all psychological babble, Gushue has two words to explain the effect of Kavanagh's plan. Gold medal. "Essentially, what we tried to do is sink a perfect performance into the subconsciousness," Kavanagh explains. It obviously worked on Brent Hamilton, whose script called for him to have a perfect game in the Canadian junior final, which he did.

To many in the sporting community, the notion of Kavanagh training the curlers to be mentally strong is puzzling. A basketball coach at every level from high school to Memorial University varsity teams, Kavanagh is considerably animated and emotional on the sidelines, akin to U.S. college hoops icon Bobby Knight. Kavanagh has been known to berate high-schoolers in full view of teammates and fans during time-outs. In fact, his two-year stint as coach of the Memorial Sea-Hawks varsity men's team, which plays in Canadian Inter-university Sport's Atlantic conference, came to a controversial end in 1991 after the players stopped just short of revolting.

"The approach I take with the curlers is not unlike any other team," Kavanagh says in defense of his coaching style. "It's just a different

Jamie Korab of Harbour Grace, shown here delivering a rock at the Players Championship, keeps everyone on the team loose. He's also, in Gushue's estimation, a world-class lead. *(Don Power/The Express photo)*

approach. In basketball, sometimes the arousal level needs to be much higher than, say, curling. They're two different sports. Would I take the same approach in football as I would with curling? Definitely not." Regardless, Gushue gives as much credit to Kavanagh for the team's success as anybody associated with the curlers. Even those in the basketball fraternity admit Kavanagh is very good at mentally preparing athletes. He even works with Newfoundland and Labrador's provincial teams.

Meanwhile, Hamilton and Adam were still eligible to curl junior in the 2001-02 season and both opted to play out their final year. Gushue and Nichols were looking for a front end when they found a pair in Gene Trickett and Paul Harvey. Trickett was forty-one, while Harvey was a few years younger. Trickett was a veteran of the Newfoundland curling scene, having played lead for Mark Noseworthy in four Briers, including the 1987 event that saw the team finish third in the Canadian championship. It was an odd mix, no doubt, a pair of twenty-one-year-olds teaming up with two curlers almost twice their age. But Gushue liked the idea of having Trickett, in particular, to bounce ideas off and discuss strategies. Trickett was a living, breathing, curling handbook. The only thing he liked better than curling was talking about curling. For Gushue, Trickett was an ideas guy. For Trickett, Gushue was a ticket to another Brier.

The new team enjoyed success early in the season, going 9-0 in the local Super League and reaching the quarter-finals in three mainland events. At the McCain SuperSpiel in New Brunswick, Gushue lost a 5-4 decision to Wayne Middaugh in the quarter-finals. While most curlers would be satisfied with the results – Gushue and Nichols were less than a year out of junior – Gushue strived for more. It couldn't be achieved, he believed, with Harvey curling second stone. In early December, Harvey was dumped from the team.

Teams routinely make changes in the off-season – the barbeque season – but it was rare to make this kind of move this early when club playdowns (the first step to determining a provincial champ) had yet to begin. "Brad had set goals for himself and if the team wasn't working, he was going to make changes," Trickett explains. "Curling was amateur and things like that traditionally didn't happen, right? But the question was: Is this the team to win? In the pros, they made trades and other moves if the fit wasn't there. That's the way Brad looked at it."

The decision to dump Harvey was met with some disgust in many local quarters. The general feeling was that St. John's was not Winnipeg, where there are literally hundreds of curlers to choose from. "I'm not too worried about that," Gushue said at the time. "Actually, I'm not worried at all." Harvey's spot was taken by Adam, who was reunited with his former teammates. But the matter was complicated because Adam was still curling junior with Ryan Ledrew, and their team was on its way to the nationals in P.E.I. As a result, the Gushue team completed a number of games – including club and zone playdowns – with just three players. Gushue did reach the provincial championship that season, but he fell short of his goal of playing in his first Brier. He lost to Mark Noseworthy in the playoffs after going 6-1 in the round-robin.

It would not be the only time Gushue would create a stir by bringing in and dropping players. The next year, Adam returned home to Wabush, Labrador, to work and pay off student loans and this time Trickett was ousted. In came Korab and Mark Ward to curl second and lead. Ward lasted two years. When the 2004-05 season opened, Korab was back in his familiar lead position and Gushue dipped into the Labrador market again, picking up veteran curler Keith Ryan, who had skipped Newfoundland's entry at the 2001 Brier. Ryan would curl for Gushue at the 2005 Brier, but the big win came in Ottawa where the Newfoundland team won the Canada Cup East and a berth in the Halifax Olympic Trials.

CURLING TERMS

HOG LINE

A line drawn across the sheet in front of the rings.

Ryan, like Trickett, Harvey, and Ward, was much older than his new teammates. He had twelve years on Gushue and Nichols and eleven on Korab. He was also married and had children. But Gushue considered the soft-spoken employee of the Iron Ore Company of Canada to be one of the finest shooters around. Ryan had reached the semifinal in the 2004 provincial championship where he lost out to Gushue. He had also played in the Masters of Curling (a World Curling Tour Grand Slam event) during the previous season in Sudbury, Ontario. So he had an idea of the competition he would be facing on a weekly basis. The main obstacle, however, was obvious. Ryan lived in Labrador, while Gushue, Nichols, and Korab were in St. John's, with a two-hour flight separating the two places. Fortunately, one of Gushue's sponsors was Air Labrador, making it easier for Ryan to join his new teammates.

Team Gushue faced a hectic schedule that season, with the Grand Slam BDO Canadian Curling Classic in Hamilton, Ontario, in October. There were also other trips on the itinerary: Regina, Saskatchewan; Bridgewater, Nova Scotia; Florenceville, New Brunswick for the McCain; and Chicoutimi, Quebec. And, of course, Gander, Newfoundland, for the Don Bartlett Classic. (The Bartlett Classic was named after the lead on Kevin Martin's rink. Don Bartlett was born in the central Newfoundland town and went to school there before heading to Edmonton, Alberta, where he eventually settled to curl while working at Canada Post.) But the big one for Team Gushue was the Canada Cup East in mid-December in Ottawa, with the coveted Trials on the line.

The hectic schedule would prove to be hard on Ryan and his family. He was in a constant juggling act between his wife and kids, his job, and his passion for curling. "I've got two young kids in different activities themselves," Ryan would say later. "They have to be carted around. Basically, my wife was a single mother when I wasn't around. And when I came home from being away, if you have problems with your delivery or something, you have to work it out. So then around eight or nine o'clock in the night, you're saying, 'Bye honey, I have to go and practice.'"

The Gushue team did receive an early Christmas gift in Ottawa in 2004, beating Ontario's Wayne Tuck 8-7 in the final at Ottawa's Rideau Curling Club. (His rink would be one of ten teams curling a year later in Halifax for a shot at representing Canada in the Winter Olympics.) After the Ottawa win, Gushue concentrated on making a third straight appearance in the Brier. He won provincials and headed to Edmonton

The Brad Gushue team won its second straight Labatt Tankard provincial championship in 2004. From left are coach Jeff Thomas, Mark Ward, Jamie Korab, Mark Nichols and Brad Gushue.
(Don Power/The Express photo)

as one of the pre-tourney favourites. But the train derailed and Gushue wound up 6-5 and out of the playoffs. Things got even worse when the team went 1-4 at the Canada Cup in Kamloops, British Columbia, immediately after the Canadian championship. The team hobbled back to Newfoundland to get ready for the grand finale of the year, the Players Championship, which is akin to the World Curling Tour's Stanley Cup or Super Bowl.

But being away from home for three weeks was too much for Ryan. He left the team and returned to Labrador City, so Gushue turned to an old reliable, Mike Adam, to throw second rock at the Players. Perhaps it was Adam, or it may have been the home cooking. Either way, it was a different Gushue team that stepped onto the ice at Mile One Stadium in downtown St. John's. Curling with a purpose that might have been missing in Edmonton and Kamloops, Gushue marched through the round-robin and registered a win over perennial contender Glenn Howard in the semifinal to set up a date against Martin in the final.

Before 5,633 fans, Martin doubled Gushue 6-3, thanks in part to a wonderful double on his last rock in the sixth end that knocked the wind from the hometown curlers and their many supporters. But chatter around the rink indicated that a second-place finish in the Players and Adam's return were no mere coincidence. Further, tongues were wagging that Gushue was prepared to make another change, especially given the fact that Ryan struggled mightily in the Brier, finishing in the bottom half of percentages among seconds. "It's all talk," said Gushue, dismissing the rumours.

Four days later, Ryan was officially out and Adam was back in as a full-time member of the team. Some would deem Gushue's decision as callous. Ryan, after all, had helped Gushue get to the Trials. Now any hopes he had of getting to the Olympics were dashed. To Gushue, never afraid to pull the trigger even if someone stood in the way, it was a business decision. "We had a comfort level at the Players with Mike," Gushue said. "Keith put in a lot of time and commitment, but the

Brad Gushue can let his hair down like anyone else, Mark Nichols says, but when he's on the ice, he's all business.
(Canadian Press photo)

chemistry just wasn't the same. We figured it would come throughout the year, but it never did."

Ryan, understandably, was crushed. He later said that given the time and commitment he devoted to curling that 2004-05 season, he could have "very easily" lost his job and, more importantly, his marriage. "Before I signed on, I checked to make sure that if we got the Olympic Trials spot would I still be there and I was told, 'Yes.' But it didn't happen." The decision to oust Ryan came at a team meeting and involved not only the curlers, but Bas Kavanagh and Toby McDonald. The question was simple: was the Gushue team good enough to win the Trials with Ryan in the lineup? The answer was unanimous.

It took a while, but Ryan said he eventually came to terms with the firing. He refused, he said, to be another Doran Johnson. Johnson, curling fans may remember, curled on Kevin Park's Edmonton team when it claimed a spot in the 1998 Olympic Trials. Like Ryan, Johnson was cut loose before the Trials. But unlike Ryan, Johnson threatened to sue Park. He even claimed he would be in Brandon, Manitoba, for the Trials with shoes and broom in hand ready to take his place on the ice, although it never happened. "I could have gone to see a lawyer," says Ryan. "I could have done a lot of things to have been a distraction for them while they were in Halifax. But I didn't because it's not my personality."

Gushue contends it was not an easy decision dropping Ward, Harvey, and Ryan. It wasn't a common practice among curling teams to make changes as they did, although this attitude may change given the success of the Newfoundlanders. This group had always taken a different view, with their trainers, their sports psychologists, and their "modern" ideas. Now they were taking a page from the professionals: if a player isn't fitting on a hockey team, the team doesn't keep him.

"You see that in every other sport except curling," Gushue says. "Why should we sacrifice a year by doing the traditional curling thing? We made

After an impressive showing at the 2004 Saskatoon Brier, plenty was expected of the Brad Gushue team in the '05 Edmonton Tim Horton Brier. But things don't always go according to plan.

(Canadian Press photo)

changes and I think they were good for the team and good for the person, too. In each situation, the person wasn't enjoying [it] and usually when you don't enjoy yourself, you don't play well. Paul and Keith weren't having fun. People came to spiels to watch us. I don't think they enjoyed that pressure."

If there was pressure in Ottawa and the Canada Cup East or at the Edmonton Brier, it wasn't holding a candle to what lay ahead in Halifax for the biggest curling event since the last Trials in Brandon. ⬤

CHAPTER 4

Toby McDonald can't help but look back and wonder why he has been so blessed. He has been in the opening credits in each of the three foremost curling stories involving Newfoundland and Canada: coach of the Gushue team that won gold in Turin, coach of the same team when they won the Olympic Trials in Halifax, and as third for Jack MacDuff's 1976 Brier-winning Newfoundland team. Until 1976, Newfoundland and Labrador had not come close to winning the Canadian men's curling championship. Their best showing in a single Brier prior to the MacDuff win was four victories since the province entered the national competition in 1951. In fact, the Newfoundland team had averaged only 1.7 wins per year.

McDonald was twenty-four in 1976 and had just been called to the bar after finishing law school. The average age of the team was only twenty-six and the four – second Doug Hudson and lead Ken Templeton were the front end – had only been together a few months. Templeton let the cat out of the bag when he talked about Newfoundland's goals in Regina on the first day of play. "We know we have to be realistic. Beating Newfoundland's past record is the most important thing."

There was no pressure on the foursome, although McDonald later admitted Templeton's hands were shaking when he got set to throw the first rock of the tournament. Newfoundland registered a pair of wins that opening day, including a 7-6 last-rock win over British Columbia's Bernie Sparkes, who won three Briers on Ron Northcott's Alberta teams and had already been inducted into the Curling Hall of Fame.

"They didn't pay too much attention to us," MacDuff said.

Matching the critics' expectations, Newfoundland dropped its next two games, including a 14-7 trouncing by Northern Ontario's Rick Lang. Had midnight come early for the Newfoundlanders? If it had indeed arrived, somebody apparently forgot to tell MacDuff, McDonald, Hudson, and Templeton. The team went on to register seven straight wins to close out the round-robin at 9-2. And a big reason for the success, McDonald said, was the team's driver, Garnet

"We're not going to bow down. No way."

- BRAD GUSHUE

"Sam" Richardson, who might have been the best curler associated with the team. Richardson curled second on Ernie Richardson's Saskatchewan curling dynasty in the late 1950s and early 1960s. The team, which also included third Arnold Richardson and lead Wes Richardson, had won four Briers between 1959 and 1962.

McDonald has said Newfoundland would not have won the Brier that year without Richardson, who passed along precious wisdom to the four wide-eyed Newfoundlanders. He was the first to teach them a corner guard: a stone off to the side of the rings, or house. Richardson was their inspiration. He supported and propped up the easterners with the confidence they needed. Even Richardson's "unorthodox" views on preparing for games were adopted by MacDuff's team.

"In the kind and sweet manner that Sam had," McDonald related to the *Edmonton Journal* a number of years later, "he convinced us that perhaps we needed to be celibate for the week, to not sleep with our wives, but sleep with each other. And while MacDuff was a nice guy, I wasn't about to cuddle up to him too much. But seriously, by the time we got to the hotel, we were bunking together because that's the way the Richardsons did it and theirs was a recipe for success as far as we were concerned."

The win by MacDuff was said to be the biggest upset ever recorded at the Brier since the first rocks were thrown in 1927. McDonald would go on to play in another three Canadian men's championships, his last coming in 1998 in Winnipeg. However, he would return again seven years later, when he coached the Brad Gushue team in Edmonton.

Jeff Thomas had coached the core of the Gushue team from 2001 to 2004 when Gushue, Nichols, Korab, and Mark Ward finished 8-4 at the Saskatoon Brier. But Thomas was finding the time commitment too heavy and told the team it was best that he step aside. Gushue immediately turned to Toby McDonald, who was regarded as

Toby McDonald played a big role in two of the greatest curling stories from Newfoundland and Labrador: he curled third on Jack MacDuff's 1976 Brier-winning team and coached the Brad Gushue Olympic gold medalists.

(Joe Gibbons/The Telegram photo)

one of the most knowledgeable curling minds in the province. McDonald agreed to take on the coaching duties, but only for the Brier. After that, he'd reevaluate, he said. He eventually agreed to come on board for the long haul because he ultimately believed he had something to offer the team.

By the time McDonald was behind the wheel, Gushue had already been to two Briers and seemed on the cusp of something big. At the 2004 nationals, he went 8-3 in Saskatoon before losing in the playoffs to Jay Peachey of British Columbia. What was left for McDonald to teach the curlers that they didn't already know? In truth, not much. But there was plenty of coaching to be done, just as Glen Sather had guided the Edmonton Oilers of the 1980s and Scotty Bowman the Montreal Canadiens of the 1970s.

One of the technical changes made by McDonald was the elimination of stopwatches, a tool widely used by most curling teams. The reason, McDonald said, was simple: he felt the Gushue team was good enough to judge weight on feel alone, that their touch on the rock and release point and eyes were good enough to determine the rock's speed. But McDonald was no fool. He was not about to step in and shake things up just for the sake of making change. His job, he explained, was to prevent them from imploding.

"People often think the only thing a coach does in curling is walk out on the ice during a time out and give the curlers some advice as to what they should do. The involvement is much more along the lines of helping one guy understand why another guy is the way he is. Perhaps he didn't mean what he said, don't take it that way, and sit down and have meetings and have everybody lay it out on the table. There's a great deal of work you do as a coach in curling, and I would expect in many other sports, that has nothing to do with being on the ice. It has to do with the attitude before you get on the ice."

After his playoff ouster in the 2002 provincial men's championship, Gushue earned his first trip to the Brier the next season in style, going 9-0 in the provincial championship. In fact, he had registered a combined 34-3 record in local Super League, club zone, and provincial playdowns for the right to represent Newfoundland and Labrador in Halifax. Gushue was excited about his first Brier, although he maintained he was not heading into his first event all awestruck and wide-eyed. "We're definitely not going in being all excited because we're playing Randy Ferbey," he said.

Gushue would finish 6-5 in Halifax following a 6-2 start. He was eyeing second place, but three straight losses to close out the round-robin dashed any playoff hopes. In the final draw, Gushue needed a win by Ontario's Brian Cochrane to force a tie-breaker, but in what would prove to be an ironic twist, Cochrane was beaten by Howard who now registered his 100th career Brier victory. Considering it was Gushue's first Brier, and he was only twenty-two, the young Newfoundlander handled it like a pro.

As coach Thomas would point out, there is much more to a Brier than curling. There are media duties and other events planned for the curlers and Gushue learned fast. "Let's face it, the Brier Patch (the curling-related party that begins early in the day and lasts long into the evening) is a good scene for a young fellow and they had to realize that," Thomas said. "But they made a pact they were there for curling and that's it."

Not that the Gushue team were, or now are, party animals. While some curling teams play hard during the day and harder at night when the lights go down, the Gushue team is often back in their rooms, getting ready for the next game. There's been many a time, Gushue has said, when other curlers have snickered at the Newfoundland goody-goodies.

A winning record aside, Gushue made quite a stir in Halifax, and not just with his shot-making. Gushue riled Ferbey when he told a reporter he wanted another crack at the reigning Brier and world champ. Gushue contends all he meant by saying he relished a rematch with the Albertan was that it would signify a playoff berth for the Newfoundlander. Ferbey didn't see it that way. "I mean, the guy's probably made $47 in his career and he's playing against guys who've won $500,000 or a million dollars and been to ten Briers," Ferbey said. "You can't be making little statements like that. Like six wins does not make a Brier. It's a long week."

Brad Gushue broke into the national men's ranks at the 2003 Nokia Brier in Halifax. Greater things would come in Halifax two years later at the Tim Hortons Olympic Trials.

(Canadian Press photo)

Gushue was quick to reply. "When you're on top, you have to expect people to challenge you. What, does he expect everybody to sit down and kneel to him just because he's Randy Ferbey? That really bothers me. I'd love to get another shot at him. He's fueled the fire now for me, for sure." The message to Ferbey and the curling world was clear: Gushue had arrived, and he was no snot-nosed, impressionable, young kid fresh out of the junior ranks. "Just the fact we were willing to say anything said a lot, I think," Gushue says. "At the time, Randy was the team and no one was willing to challenge him. But we were. I wanted another crack because I felt if we played as well as we could, we could have beaten him."

Gushue's feelings on the subject have not changed. "Still, to this day, we're one of the teams willing to challenge him and go head to head. If he beats us, he beats us. And if he doesn't, good for us. You see it in golf, too, when people [compete] with Tiger [Woods]. Most of them fold. There are very few willing to go eye-to-eye with him down the stretch. We are willing to go eye-to-eye with Randy. We've come out on the lower end of it more than the upper end, but I think we did send a message to him that we are one of those teams. We've made some other comments over the years that let people know just because you're from Alberta or Manitoba, we're not going to bow down. No way."

Fueled by that desire, Gushue was intent on getting another shot at the Brier. The 2004 championship was set for Saskatoon's SaskPlace and, if nothing else, the province had proven to be a lucky charm for Newfoundland curlers. Meanwhile, the provincials that year were set for mid-February in Goose Bay, Labrador, which created a

> "What, does he expect everybody to sit down and kneel to him just because he's Randy Ferbey?
>
> - BRAD GUSHUE

dilemma for Korab. In January, during a Super Bowl party at a downtown St. John's bar, Korab won two tickets to Hawaii and a pair of seats for the NFL's Pro Bowl game. However, taking the trip would mean missing a week of practice and possibly the opening draw at the provincials.

Korab admitted it took him a couple of hours to make a decision. Curling in frigid Labrador or a free trip to Hawaii, football tickets, and a free hotel? "After talking to everybody, I came to the decision we'd worked too hard to let a distraction or something that could affect the outcome of our provincials get in the way," Korab said. "It's a twenty-four-hour trip to get from Honolulu to St. John's and then on to Goose Bay. It just would have been too hard. I can always buy a trip to Hawaii to watch the Pro

Bowl. I can't buy a trip to play in the Brier." So as the NFLers gathered in 32°C Hawaii, Korab joined his teammates in Goose Bay where the temperatures dipped to -60°C. In fact, the provincial final between Gushue and Mark Noseworthy had to be postponed for a day when the lights went out at the Goose Bay Curling Club due to the intense cold.

Gushue eventually beat Noseworthy to earn a second straight trip to the Brier. After three draws in Saskatoon, Randy Ferbey, who was coming off a third straight Brier title, and Russ Howard, making his thirteenth start in the nationals, were tied atop the leader board at 3-0. Joining them was Gushue, which surprised many of the spectators. But not Gushue. "Russ and Randy, they're extremely hard workers and they put a lot into it, and the one thing I'm really known for in Newfoundland is being a hard worker, and I think those sorts of things pay off," he explained. "I throw more rocks than anybody in Newfoundland, and I'm willing to bet most players in Canada. I love the game and I love practicing. Throwing rocks is my sanctuary."

The foursome arrived in Saskatoon as prepared as any team, having played a full World Curling Tour schedule on a $40,000 budget, money that not only came from sponsors but out of the curlers' own pockets as well. Once again, the Gushue team was the youngest in the field with an average age of twenty-seven. But that number was raised considerably by the presence of their 40-year-old lead, the lanky Mark Ward, who held the broom for Gushue while Korab, the second, and Nichols swept. With two games to play to close out the round-robin, Gushue was tied with Howard at 7-2 for third place. One of those games was a rematch with Ferbey. But the much-heralded showdown didn't pan out. Ferbey wiped the ice with Gushue in an 11-3 thumping. Gushue had beaten Quebec earlier in the day to finish 8-3 and secure a tie-breaker, although this was little consolation. Had he beaten Ferbey, Gushue would have finished second and gained an extra playoff life.

Gushue was set to play British Columbia's Jay Peachey in Saturday's tie-breaker. It was a game of enormous proportions because not only was the winner moving on to the semifinal, the team was also gaining a berth in the Olympic Trials. The other two curlers still in contention – Ferbey and Nova Scotia's Mark Dacey – had already secured spots in the Trials. Ferbey earned a trip to Halifax after winning the 2003 Strauss Canada Cup, while Dacey was runner-up at the 2003 Brier.

The Gushue-Peachey game also had a delicious subplot given what had developed in their earlier round-robin meeting, which Gushue won handily 8-1. In that game, Peachey angered Gushue by asking the Newfoundland skip to move from the house while the British Columbia team discussed strategy. "I was, for the first time in the Brier, treated like a child," Gushue said. "It wasn't what was said, but rather the context in which it was said. It was condescending and I'm sure it wouldn't have been said that way to Russ Howard, for example. Maybe he [Peachey] figured he could say it that way because I'm only twenty-three. But we've been here before and I think we've earned respect that wasn't shown in that instance."

In the tie-breaker, Gushue was down 6-5 in the tenth end with last rock. When it came down to the final four shots, Newfoundland had two rocks buried in the four-foot. Then Peachey, who looks every bit the accountant he is, delivered what would be deemed the shot of the week on his final throw. The New Westminster curler made a difficult bump-back, pushing the Newfoundland stone back slightly and rolling a few inches to bite the four-foot for shot rock, the stone that's scoring. Gushue was left with a difficult angle-raise double takeout for two points and the win, but his final delivery over-curled and left Peachey with a steal of one and the win.

Afterwards, when Gushue met with reporters, his eyes welled with tears. "It's pretty devastating because Olympic Trials spots are hard to come by and every chance you get, you need to take it because you don't know when you're going to get another one," he said. "It sucks that I miscalled that last one," he added, after calling Korab and Nichols off the shot instead of letting them take it down the ice. "That's what really hurts the most. I had it made out of my hand. I let the guys down on that one." Gushue won first-team all-star honours at the tournament, while Nichols and Korab were voted to the second all-star team.

The 2004-05 season brought a new look to the team when Ryan came aboard to replace Ward. Part of the reason for adding Ryan was that Gushue considered him one of the finest shooters in the province. The other part was Gushue's wish to have Korab curl lead. Gushue and Co.

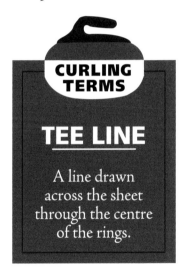

CURLING TERMS

TEE LINE

A line drawn across the sheet through the centre of the rings.

had a hectic schedule planned, and the whole season, he said, was geared towards Ottawa and the Canada Cup East bonspiel in mid-December. The Ottawa and Rideau curling clubs were playing host to twenty-eight teams for the Canada Cup East and a $98,000 purse. But for most of the curlers, the carrot dangling at the end of the stick was a berth in the Halifax Olympic Curling Trials.

Gushue's team entered the event ranked fourth and, as a result, earned a first-round bye. Their first game was against Nova Scotia's Shawn Adams, and the Newfoundlanders got an early jump, leading 5-1 after four ends. But the wheels fell off as Adams scored two in the fifth and stole three in the next end on the way to a 9-7 win. Gushue rebounded with three straight wins but lost 6-5 to Ontario's Peter Corner, dropping him to the C final with one last chance to make the championship round. A 7-4 decision over

Dean Joanisse of British Columbia set up a quarter-final rematch with Corner which Gushue won by another 7-4 count.

Next was a semifinal game against Ontario's Wayne Middaugh, whom Gushue had failed to beat in three meetings. He picked the perfect time to register his first win, edging Howard's former second 5-4 in an extra end. That set up a final against another Ontario curler, Wayne Tuck, who entered the event ranked twenty-fourth but managed to dodge all kinds of bullets in his improbable run. Gushue fell behind 3-0 after two ends before getting two points back in the third. He pulled ahead with a deuce in the fourth and it was back and forth after that. Gushue trailed 7-6 heading home, but had last-shot advantage. With a lot of rocks in play, Tuck faced a tough cross-the-house double takeout which would have forced Gushue to draw for the single and force the extra end. However, the London, Ontario, curler missed the double, leaving Gushue with a draw to the eight foot for the win. He dropped his last shot right on the button. The Gushue team was handed a $12,000 first-place cheque, and while the money was nice, it was a Trials berth that meant the most. The Trials were, said Gushue, the hardest event to get into in the country.

After returning home, the team set its sights on the seventy-sixth Brier, although that would be anticlimactic given the Ottawa win. Dave Nedohin, who throws last rock for Ferbey, maintains that the Brier is still where it's at – especially after the Ferbey team's miserable performance at the Halifax Trials just before Christmas of 2005. Gushue begs to differ. "Don't get me wrong, the Brier is still a huge event. But the Olympics, that's the pinnacle," Gushue says. "The Brier, in my opinion, is the second-biggest event next to the Olympics. Right now, our main concern is being as prepared as we can for December [and Halifax]."

Gushue, Nichols, Ryan, and Korab made it a three-peat at the provincial championship in early February, 2005, beating Noseworthy in the Labatt Tankard all-Newfoundland and Labrador championship game for the second straight year. Both had finished 7-2 in the round-robin and one of Gushue's losses was an 8-6 setback to Noseworthy. A mid-week lineup change saw Adam replace Korab as lead after the latter had come down with a bout of the flu. "Mike's enthusiasm sparked us," Gushue said. But he quickly added that Korab would be back in the lead's position at the Brier.

Despite the fine showing at the provincials in Corner Brook, Gushue had not been playing well on the national stage. He was 1-3 at the Canadian Open in Winnipeg, although the skip pointed out that two of those losses were last-shot setbacks to Kevin Martin and Glenn Howard. When the Newfoundland curlers touched down in Edmonton for the 2005 Brier, it wasn't long before Nichols again established himself as one of the finest shooters in Canada before the Brier even opened. He beat out some of the game's top curlers – including Ferbey, Middaugh, and Ferbey's second, Scott Pfeifer – to win the Ford Hot Shots title.

The Hot Shots is a chance for curlers to compete against each other in individual skills competitions. Before the first draw of the Brier, four curlers from each participating province make six shots – hit and stick, draw to the button, draw the port, the raise, hit and roll, and double takeout – in the preliminary round, with the top eight advancing to the quarter-finals. Nichols climbed his way to the top and won a two-year lease valued at $13,600 on a new Ford Five Hundred SEL, a snappy new five-passenger sedan. For Team Gushue, it was to be the only highlight of the Brier.

To the casual curling fan, the Edmonton Brier looked to be a weak field. There was Ferbey, of course, seeking his fourth title in five years, and Middaugh, a two-time Brier champ, and world champion with Howard. But who knew of Manitoba's Randy Dutiaume or Adams or Deane Horning from British Columbia? As a result, Gushue was picked in some corners to win Newfoundland's second Brier. Mike Harris, the Olympic silver medalist in Nagano and a CBC commentator, said at the Scott Tournament of Hearts that Ferbey and Middaugh were the teams to beat, but Gushue was part of a strong second tier. He proved in the opening draw that this speculation was, in fact, dead on.

Gushue's team registered a dramatic 11-10 decision over Northern Ontario's Mike Jakubo. Trailing 10-9 with hammer, Gushue had to oust a Northern Ontario stone scoring in the four-foot and buried behind a handful of guards. But Gushue delivered a beautiful off-in shot with his last rock, knocking in a stone in the outer 12-foot ring, skimming past one of his own, and taking out the Northern Ontario shot rock out to count two points for the win. Gushue lost his next start, 10-6 to Ferbey, but remained undaunted. "They're only a team. Four guys. The rocks don't know Randy Ferbey is throwing them. People get caught up in that, but we don't look at it as playing Randy Ferbey ... we're playing the eight rocks that are being thrown," he said.

Meanwhile, Ferbey was far more complimentary. "Brad, he's twenty-four and I think when all is said and done he's going to have more [purple] hearts [as Brier champ] than anybody who's going to play this game." Sporting a 4-1 record through five games, the wheels fell off in a pair of one-point losses to Adams and Horning, and Newfoundland could not rebound. Gushue's front end of Korab and Ryan, especially, had been the subject of criticism from the CBC's Harris and Joan McCusker, who both said Gushue and Nichols were left with far too many difficult shots because Korab and Ryan were not carrying their end of the bargain. "We're missing shots, throwing draws through the house and missing open hits," Gushue said. "We're playing awful."

The next day, Gushue dropped a third straight game to Quebec, but rebounded to beat Saskatchewan to improve to 5-4. That meant Gushue had to register wins over Dutiaume and Middaugh in his last two round-robin games to secure even a tie-breaker. He got by the Manitoba curler

8-6 in the afternoon. Then, that night, he watched Middaugh score four points in the seventh end en route to a 7-5 victory, dropping Gushue to a 6-5 record. It didn't get any better at the Strauss Canada Cup of Curling a couple of days later in Kamloops, British Columbia, where Gushue staggered to a 1-4 record. A tournament by invite only, Gushue qualified after winning the Canada Cup East. He would lose to Harris, then Ferbey for the second time in less than a week, and then Jeff Stoughton and Mark Dacey. His only win was a 9-7 decision over Pat Ryan. For their efforts, the team took home $750. Gushue and Co. had failed to pocket enough cash in Kamloops for even a single flight home to St. John's. It was time for a dramatic turnaround. ●

CHAPTER 5

The Gushue team made up for Kamloops and their disappointing showing at the Brier with an outstanding effort at the 2005 Players Championship, staged in their own backyard at Mile One Stadium in St. John's. After losing to Kevin Martin in the Players final, the Gushue curlers still pocketed a handsome payout of $30,000. For the team, however, it was the final result and not the money that made all the difference. And Gushue made it known that Adam played a huge part in the outcome. The writing was also on the wall for Ryan.

"The thing with Mike is that the four of us are best friends and it's such an easy fit," Gushue said at the time. "We have curled together so much and get along so well, chemistry does not become an issue. All of us played well. We played as a team, more than we did the last couple of weeks."

Gushue registered three wins against world-class teams to open the World Curling Tour's season finale: a 9-4 decision over defending champ John Morris of Calgary in the opener; an 8-1 win over Sweden's Peja Lindholm, a three-time world champ; and a 6-3 decision over Winnipeg's Jeff Stoughton, a two-time Brier winner and a former world champion. Gushue dropped a 6-5 decision to Pete Fenson of the United States in his fourth start, but came back with a 5-3 win over Pat Simmons of

Saskatchewan to close out the round-robin 4-1. After a 9-8 quarter-final win over Switzerland's Ralph Stoeckli (a game in which Gushue scored a startling five points in the fifth end), the hometown team slipped past Glenn Howard of Ontario 7-6 in the semifinal when Gushue stole the winning point in the 10th end.

Meanwhile, Martin was stringing together a bunch of wins himself, setting the stage for an East-West showdown. The final on Easter Sunday was close through five ends, but Martin picked up three points in the sixth to knock the stuffing out of the Mile One crowd of 5,633 on the way to a 6-3 win. Not even the live music between ends from the band Siochana, made up of police officers from the Royal Newfoundland Constabulary, could jumpstart the Gushue faithful. "Before the game started, when the band played that song 'I'm Proud to be an Islander,' with everyone clapping, that was very cool," Gushue said. "We are never going to have an opportunity to have a Brier here, not in the near future anyway. So this is as close as it would get and I was glad to be part of it."

In Russ Howard, the Gushue team was adding a Hall of Famer and the career leader in wins at the Brier.

(Joe Gibbons/The Telegram photo)

So with less than a year before the opening of the Olympic Trials, Gushue closed out the 2004-05 season on a high note – the Players Championship finish and the Canada Cup East outcome sandwiching disappointing results in the Brier and Canada Cup. But even though the season was over, he was still making news. Four days after the Players Championship, Adam was officially back in as Gushue's second and Ryan was out. Bigger news came less than a week later when Gushue, Nichols, Adam, Korab, and coach McDonald added Russ Howard as fifth man. Now the curling world was *really* buzzing.

Russell Winston Howard is perhaps the most decorated curler in Canada. His 107 victories remain a Brier record, as does his thirteen appearances as skip in the Canadian men's championship. A two-time Brier and world champion, Howard was already a Curling Hall of Famer and, according to *Sweep!* magazine, the curler of the century when Gushue came knocking. His grip on the game was so strong that he was included in *The Globe and Mail's* list of the top twenty-five most powerful and influential personalities in Canadian sport in 1994, just behind Cliff Fletcher, then president and general manager of the Toronto Maple Leafs. Howard had long been an idol of Brad Gushue. His trademark "Hurry harrrrrrd!," like the cry of a bear in search of a snack, had captivated the young St. John's curler. Now Howard had become a free agent after his team from New Brunswick failed to win a berth in the 2005 Trials.

In the 2001 Olympic qualifier, Howard finished 5-4 after going 3-6 in 1997. Howard was even around in 1987, finishing 4-3 at the Trials won by Ed Lukowich, who would curl in the 1988 Calgary Olympics when it was just a demonstration sport. The Ontario native was a fierce competitor on the ice, a "Crusty Rusty" who hated – no, thoroughly despised – losing. Gushue liked that trait. "He brings so much to the table," says Gushue. "He brings a winning attitude. He doesn't accept losing. Our concern," he adds, "was would he accept the offer? You are asking a guy who was voted curler of the century to be fifth man, so you don't know what he is going to say." As it happens, Howard jumped at the opportunity.

Howard was born in Midland, Ontario, a town described as the "gateway to Georgian Bay's picturesque 30,000 islands," about an hour and a half north of Toronto. He threw his first curling rock at eleven, and when the curling season was over, Howard would turn to golf. In fact, he made a career out of the sport, working as the golf pro at Midland's Brooklea course. He went to Brooklea the day after graduating from Georgian College in Barrie, Ontario, and stayed for twenty-six years.

In some corners of Canada, golf and curling attract society's upper crust, but Howard grew up in a very middle-class home with his parents, Bill and Barb, and younger brother, Glenn. It was from his father, who passed away in 2003, that Howard got his competitive streak. The elder Howard lived by the rule that if you went at something, you went at it 100 %. And nothing stood in his way. At seventy-two, Bill Howard built his own cottage from scratch, and this after suffering a heart attack. Immediately after leaving hospital, he purchased a ten-speed bike to whip himself into shape. "I got my intensity, everything, from my dad," Russ says. "He was a very focused individual, very intense. He tried his best at everything, didn't matter what it was." Barb Howard is still going strong at eighty-four, although a hip operation in the spring of 2006 has slowed her a little.

> "I can safely say I've spent more money curling than I've made."
>
> - RUSS HOWARD

At twenty-three, Russ curled in his first Brier with Kent Carstairs, Bob Ruston, and Larry Merkley in 1980 at the Calgary Corral, where he finished 5-6 for Ontario. "I was twenty-three and wet behind the ears," he explained to the *Calgary Herald*. "I was watching Paul Gowsell and Rick Folk and Al Hackner. Nobody knew who Al Hackner was ... nobody knew who we were either. That was a long time ago. It was a great, great event."

It would be six years before Howard would get to another Brier, but he made the best of it. In 1986 in Kitchener-Waterloo, Howard finished runner-up to Alberta's Lukowich. The next year, with his younger brother, Glenn, at third and Tim Belcourt and Kent Carstairs on the front end, Howard would lose only two games in Edmonton en route to his first Canadian men's championship. At the world championship in Vancouver, he would only lose twice again in winning Canada's sixth championship in seven years. Howard made three more attempts at the Brier – finishing second in 1992 and third in 1989 – before recapturing his winning form at the 1993 Ottawa Labatt Brier with his brother throwing third stone and Wayne Middaugh and Peter Corner at the front end. He would later earn another world crown for Canada in Geneva, Switzerland, in early April 1993.

Howard has skipped some great teams. In 1998, the year before he left Ontario to move to New Brunswick, the Howard foursome of Glenn Howard, Corner, and Neil Harrison (Middaugh would form his own team, which would win the 1998 Brier and world championship) won $143,000, tops in Canada and breaking the barrier for most single-season earnings by a curling team. The team that won the 1993 Brier and worlds was unique, he says. "I'm biased, but I think it was the best team that ever played. Ferbey's teams may be proving otherwise, but certainly when I played we were pretty unstoppable. There was one season we only lost six games the whole year. We won over $100,000 four years in a row, and that was back between 1991-94. That's a lot of money. It was a hell of a team."

In hindsight, Howard says he did it all wrong early in his career. He was content, he said, just to curl locally. He didn't understand that to get better, he had to attract the better curlers and, perhaps most importantly, had to get away from the Midland curling scene and explore the big wide world. "In '86 when we lost the Brier final, we'd won just $2,000 curling that year," he said. "But all of a sudden, when Glenn got old enough and good enough, I had a real good team. We came second and started getting invited to these big spiels and that opened my eyes."

At the 1993 Canadian championship, Howard beat Rick Folk of Kelowna, British Columbia, 5-3 in the final at the Civic Centre in a game that lacked excitement. "The fans are right," Howard said afterwards. "It was boring." Typical, in other words, of the game that curling had become. Curling through the late 1980s and early 1990s had devolved into a game of place a rock, remove a rock. If a team picked up a point or two early on, the remainder of the game was spent knocking out the other team's rocks. The peel game, where curlers peeled off or removed each others' stones, had become curling's buzz word.

Of all Howard's accomplishments, from the Brier and world titles, to the World Curling Tour championships and Skins Game wins, to the boatload of cash he's earned over the years, one of his proudest accomplishments, he says, has been the development of the Moncton Rule, also known as the free guard zone, or four rock rule. "Everybody was hitting and [the] ice in the arenas was straight so you could easily win 1-0 in the Briers," he said. "Although it took some skill to throw the peels, it wasn't too exciting to watch. It was right beside watching paint dry for excitement."

Howard began to wonder, what if the first four rocks had to remain in play? Top of the twelve-foot, back of the house, on the button … it didn't matter. He tried a couple of dry runs with his brother, Glenn, in practice and put it to the test in 1991 at the Moncton 100, a bonspiel that attracted some of the world's top teams. "The Europeans fell in love with it and adopted it immediately, and the very next year they adopted it everywhere in the world except Canada."

After tinkering with Howard's creation, the free guard zone was introduced into the 1994 Labatt Brier. "It took some more research, but the Canadian Curling Association came up with the same concept, and from that point on we have a free guard zone where the first four rocks cannot be removed," Howard explained. "It's created a tremendous following, I think. It's so much more exciting for the crowd and the players. I'm pretty proud of that, actually."

But Howard and the CCA were not always on the same page when it came to curling issues. His clash with the sport's governing body over the players' right to earn money over sponsorship crests was one of Howard's most public battles. In early 1995, Howard joined forces with twenty-six other curlers, including the great Ed "The Wrench" Werenich of Toronto who was twice a Brier and world champ, to ask the Ontario courts to discard the CCA's dress code at provincial and national championships. The CCA restricted curlers to wearing only crests that represented the major sponsor at the event. Curlers at the national women's championship – the Scott Tournament of Hearts – could only don Scott-related cresting. Likewise for the men at the Labatt Brier.

"The only negativism I hear is, 'Oh, you just want to get rich,'" Howard told the *Edmonton Journal* in November, 1995. "Well, that's never going to happen. I can safely say I've spent more money curling than I've made. I want Canada to be a dominant curling force forever, and I don't think that's going to happen. Europeans have sponsorships, they can wear sponsorship crests on television, and some of them are funded to come over to our spiels and learn against the best."

Despite their apparent resolve, Howard and Co. never even made it to court. The players withdrew their fight, after some of the dissidents backed off. Heather Houston, a two-time Scott Tournament of Hearts winner, and teammate Lorraine Lang were preparing for the 1996 Scott and it was hinted that their association with Howard, Werenich, et al., could influence Scott's support of the Canadian women's championship. "She turtled," was the way Werenich put it in describing Houston. It would take about ten years, but eventually the curlers and the CCA would reach a resolution on the cresting issue. It was, like the Moncton Rule, one of Howard's proudest moments.

"What really happened there," Howard says today, "was we won in 1993 and at my second worlds, we were deluged with opportunities for sponsors and stuff. We had a deal with Ford. They were going to give us four automobiles and then they realized they couldn't put Ford on our backs for us to wear at the Brier on TV. The whole deal went south. We said, 'That's crazy. What the hell? Why can't we wear a crest?' And me being in the golf industry, I'm watching Jack Nicklaus and the others heavily, heavily sponsored. Lee Trevino's favourite line was he played on the PGA Tour to make enough money to pay the taxes on his endorsements."

The issue wasn't decided without a messy clash that had Howard smack dab in the middle. In 1999, Howard and his family packed their bags and moved from Ontario to Moncton, New Brunswick, where he had accepted a job as the director of golf and sales at the exclusive Royal Oaks Golf Club in Moncton, a career that lasted four years until housing sales on the course slowed to a crawl and he elected to join his wife, Wendy, as a Moncton realtor. Starting in 1999, Howard would win five of six New Brunswick provincial championships, with 2001 snapping the streak of a half-dozen straight appearances at the Brier. But he still made it to the nationals that year, working as a colour commentator for TSN.

The year 2001 also marked the formation of the World Curling Tour's Grand Slam of Curling, a four-event series of bonspiels with a total purse of almost $500,000. The Slam was backed by International Management Group (IMG) and bankrolled with a big television deal with Sportsnet. The Slam would be staged throughout the 2001-02 season, competing directly with provincial playdowns for the Brier. The Tour, led by World Curling Players Association president Kevin Martin, insisted that teams sign contracts barring them from playing non-sanctioned televised events such as the Brier. In addition to Martin and Howard, other former Brier winners such as Wayne Middaugh, Kerry Burtnyk, Jeff Stoughton, and Vic Peters added their names to the list.

The players still wanted to have a pro-like curling tour from September to April. They wanted to stage all provincial championships at the same time so more weekend dates were open for Tour cash spiels. And they wanted to allow top-ranked Tour teams a free ride into provincial championships, bypassing club and zone championships and the like. Then there was that business of permitting curlers to wear sponsorship crests at provincial and national championships. The curlers, in reality, wanted a larger slice of the Brier pie.

There were a few top-shelf teams, namely Randy Ferbey's and John Morris's foursomes, who elected not to sign the Tour's agreement and were barred from the cash spiels. Clearly, lines were drawn in the sand and the message was simple: you're either with us or you're not. "It's very important for the players that we build our tour," Martin said. "They really don't care," said David Nedohin, who tossed last rocks for Ferbey's team. "They just feel that we're

CURLING TERMS

BONSPIEL

A curling tournament.

not being supportive, and therefore there should be a penalty. I think it's absolutely absurd."

If Ferbey's and Morris's choices not to join the Slammers created a ripple, Russ Howard invoked a tidal wave in the fall of 2001 when he said he would defy the Tour by entering the New Brunswick Brier playdowns. It was in direct conflict of what the Tour had said was a "legally binding contract." Howard left a small window open by saying he would play in the first two Slam stops in Wainwright, Alberta, and Gander, Newfoundland, in the New Year. In truth, he had tried to renege on his entire Slam obligation, but he felt guilty when he learned the Sportsnet television deal could fall apart if he pulled out. Howard felt it was unreasonable to suggest the four Grand Slam events and Brier playdowns could not coincide.

"I have a [feeling in the] pit [of] in my stomach," he told the *Calgary Herald*. "They're basically taking all the high-priced talent and wiping out the Brier, and nobody can convince me that's good for the game." He was also upset that the Tour banned Ferbey and Morris from its events for refusing to sign on. Howard missed the inaugural Slam event in Wainwright because of a family commitment, and he didn't even get the chance to curl in Gander. That's because the World Curling Tour slapped him with a two-year suspension from the four Slams just a day after playing in the opening round of his provincial playdowns early in 2002.

"It just doesn't make any sense at all," Howard told the *Moncton Times and Transcript*. "All we've been doing as a small-town team from New Brunswick is trying to do the right thing for curling. Nobody can convince me that boycotting the Brier is the right thing to do." The World Curling Tour's then-executive director Chad McMullan hinted his group was exploring legal action. "This is not going to slide, I guarantee you that," he promised. Howard was also contemplating legal advice to recoup money spent on airline tickets to Newfoundland. Howard would go on to win the New Brunswick provincials and play in the Calgary Brier. In an ironic twist, he reached the semifinal only to be beaten by Morris. Morris would then lose to Ferbey in the final.

"The curlers have been given a better deal since I was fighting for it ten years ago," Howard said in Calgary. "When I was worrying about sponsorship and stuff like that, the curlers were getting $4,000 or $5,000. Now we get something like $16,000 or $17,000, and your expenses – your flights, rooms, and food – are paid and you get a huge per diem. The Brier is a good event." No legal action was taken by either side, but it was clear the whole thing had left a sour taste in Kevin Martin's mouth, despite Howard's contention that they remained "friends."

At the Don Bartlett Classic in the fall of 2002, Martin, after acknowledging that talk of a truce between the Canadian Curling

Association and the World Curling Tour was progressing, said: "The game was going nowhere. But thank goodness there were players with the wherewithal to stick together and make the changes. As for the players who didn't come with us, are there any ill feelings? No. But I think the big guns who didn't come with us, there's no question twenty years from now they'll know they goofed. In their hearts they have to know they let their peers down, and any time you let your peers down, I think that's a problem. They'll have to look at themselves in the mirror."

In the spring of 2003, the CCA and WCT came to an agreement, one that wasn't made official until September. The WCT voided any contracts that players signed keeping them from non-sanctioned events and promised to schedule its cash spiels around CCA events and provincial playdowns. In return, the CCA encouraged all provincial associations to stage their playdowns at the same time. But perhaps most importantly, there was an agreement on the age-old cresting argument. Cresting positions on team uniforms would be sold, generating an anticipated $150,000 and each Brier team getting $10,000 in cresting income. The top four teams would also receive a larger cash prize. Coincidentally, only one team that had signed and stuck with the Slammers reached the 2004 Brier. And Saskatchewan's Bruce Korte finished 5-6.

It may have cost them a few trips to the Brier, but the dissident curlers had managed to secure what they wanted – Brier prize money, sponsorship cresting, and standardized scheduling of provincial playdowns.

Somewhere in New Brunswick, Russ Howard was smiling. ●

CHAPTER 6

Just as they had done five years earlier, the Brad Gushue curling team resigned themselves to an off-season of hard work in the summer of 2005. Winning the Canadian and world junior men's championships were one thing. Toppling the best in the game at the Olympic Trials and reserving a trip to Turin, Italy, and the 20th edition of the Winter Olympic Games was something else.

All four curlers took a page from other pro athletes and began to tone their bodies, secure in the knowledge that while the opposition might be better, they wouldn't be in better condition. To whip themselves into shape, they again turned to a Memorial University professor, Dave Behm, a kinesiologist and exercise physiologist who designed a specific program for the needs of this sport. The curlers each spent upwards of two hours a day in the gym and, in a scene straight out of "Rocky" when the Italian Stallion runs the steps at Philadelphia's Museum of Art, Gushue and his fellow curlers were sprinting the 100 steep steps behind Mile One Stadium every day. Unlike Rocky Balboa, however, they didn't celebrate with a victory dance. That would come later in Halifax and Italy. So would memories of the exercise program. "We were staying on the fifth floor of the [Olympic] Village," recalled Korab, "and I was walking up the stairs complaining about the forty steps I had to walk versus the 5,000 I ran in one day last summer."

"I put on eight pounds and increased my strength 100 per cent," Gushue said at the time of the heavy workouts. "The improvement has been unbelievable. All of us have increased muscle, and overall we just feel great about ourselves." In fact, he discovered muscles he never knew existed. So serious was Gushue about the training that he spent very little time on Newfoundland's golf courses. Jamie Korab also relinquished one of his favourite pastimes when he took the season off from soccer. A talented goalkeeper, Korab was the backup on the provincial championship team in 2004 that represented Newfoundland and Labrador at the men's nationals.

Korab hailed from the small community of Harbour Grace, about an hour's drive from St. John's. He tossed his first curling stone at the Conception Bay North Curling Club, which has since closed its doors, and as he progressed through the ranks, he would often make the round trip to the capital city to play his junior games at the St. John's Curling Club. Before leaving for Turin, Korab made sure to visit a St. John's hair salon to have a touch of red dye added to his mane.

Jamie Korab likes to have fun, Brad Gushue admits. Having different personalties on a team is important to winning, he said.

(Joe Gibbons/The Telegram photo)

"He is different," acknowledges Gushue. "If you had four Brad Gushues, you wouldn't win a game. If you had four Mark Nichols, you wouldn't win a game. [Korab's] attitude on the ice loosens me and Mark up. When Jamie's at his best, he makes me and Mark better. It's not so much him curling ninety-five per cent but his attitude that makes me and

Mark play better. He makes us feel loose and confident. The off-ice stuff, he is what he is. Jamie is very one-track. If he goes to the Brier Patch, he's just worried about having a good time, hob-nobbing. If I go there, I'm still thinking about two days ahead."

But Gushue is also quick to point out that he considers Korab a world-class lead. It's why the switch was made to have him throw the first two rocks after the 2004 Brier. In the world of curling, the lead stone is akin to the Witness Protection Program. Of the three Briers that Korab has appeared in, he's been interviewed only once by the media. It came at the 2005 Edmonton event when a reporter asked what the weather was like in Newfoundland. "I told him it was snowing, and that was it," Korab shrugs. "So for three Briers, the only interview I had was, 'What's the weather like?' I think it was more of a question than an interview. But it was a reporter who asked me, so I count it."

In this game, it's the skip who gets all the glory. But if he misses last shot, he shoulders all the blame, too. The third picks up the media scraps. Leads and seconds are like hockey's second-line defensive centers, or the sure-handed, light-hitting shortstops. Nobody notices, except teammates. "And I'm screwed on this team," said Korab. "Mark throws the big weight and gets appreciation for that and people know him for that. Russ holds the broom and gets recognition for that, plus the fact he's a Hall of Famer. And Brad gets recognition because he throws the last rock. Then you add me into the mix, who throws the first two rocks and then sweeps the rest of the way."

Still, a winning team, says Howard, is a team that's solid one through four. And the key to a strong front end are players who want to curl lead or second. "Mark my words," he says, "look back at the best teams in the world, the teams that were the hottest and I'll show you a good front end, and I'll show you curlers who want to play front end. Neil Harrison [who won a Brier and world title with Ed Werenich in 1983] wanted to be a

Brad Gushue started
curling at age thirteen.
His last game of hockey was
the day before his first game of curling.
(Joe Gibbons/The Telegram photo)

career lead. He wanted to learn the position and be good at it. That's the trick to a world-class team. You need to have a good skip and a good vice [vice skip, or third], but nowadays it takes four players. Take [Marcel] Rocque and [Scott] Pfeifer with Randy Ferbey. They don't want to play skip or vice. Pfeifer could skip just about any team in Alberta, but he wants to be second stone. That's part of the secret to any great team."

Gushue, Nichols, Adam, and Korab had a busy schedule planned through the fall of 2005 as they prepared for the Trials that would open on December 3 at the Halifax Metro Centre, site of their first Brier. And the season started early, on September 16, across the big pond in Oslo, Norway. In Scandinavia, the Gushue team would curl in two events, beginning with the Bompi Cup, a tune-up for the Oslo Cup, which attracted bigger, more "name" teams.

Gushue got off to a strong start, going 5-0 to win the Bompi Cup, and then he extended his unbeaten record to eight games with three straight victories in the round-robin portion of the Oslo Cup.

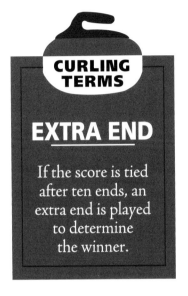

CURLING TERMS

EXTRA END

If the score is tied after ten ends, an extra end is played to determine the winner.

The Oslo event attracted most of Europe's top teams: local hero Pal Trulsen, the reigning Olympic gold medalist from Norway; Sweden's Peja Lindholm; Markku Uusipaavalniemi of Finland; Switzerland's Ralph Stoeckli; Andreas "Andy" Kapp of Germany; and Dave Murdoch of Scotland. All six would curl in the Olympic Games. But Gushue's streak was snapped in the first game of the playoffs with an 8-2 loss to Sweden's Nils Carlsen. The loss would mark the start of a downward spiral for Team Gushue.

Next on the agenda was the Don Bartlett Classic in Gander, a central Newfoundland town about four hours from St. John's. The field for "The Bartlett," as it's known, was not as strong as previous years, although it still attracted the likes of Scotland's Murdoch, and Canada's Kevin Martin, Wayne Middaugh, Glenn Howard, Shawn Adams, and Guy Hemmings.

Gushue won his first game in Gander, defeating Hemmings 6-5 in 10 ends. Hemmings had burst onto the national curling scene in 1998 and 1999 with a pair of second-place finishes at the Brier. His trademark quickly became the unkempt "bed head" look, and Hemmings endeared himself to fans with an outgoing, playful personality. Privately, some curlers suggest it's all an act. When the television cameras are off, Hemmings is not shy to slam a broom, and when Gushue was a youngster fresh out of the junior ranks Hemmings virtually ignored the Newfoundlander on the ice when the two met in World Curling Tour events. Yet despite his lack of results, Hemmings is one of the Canadian Curling Association's pitch men with his "Rockin' The House Tour."

Gushue lost 8-6 to eventual champion Middaugh in his next game, but rebounded with wins over a pair of Newfoundland curlers and Ontario's Chad Allen to finish 3-2 and secure a spot in the tie-breaker with three other teams. But Gushue would be ousted with losses to Murdoch and Pierre Charette of Quebec. Five days later, the curlers were off to Bonnyville, Alberta, and the result was much the same, a 3-3 record and out of the playoffs. Team Gushue continued their road trip to The National, the first of four Grand Slam events.

It was in Port Hawkesbury, Nova Scotia, that Russ Howard was inserted into the lineup in place of Adam at second stone. The new-look team went 3-2 in the round-robin, beating Uusipaavalniemi, Lindholm, and Murdoch, but they were not so lucky against Trulsen and Jeff Stoughton. Gushue lost his quarter-final game 9-5 to Ferbey even though he led 3-1 after three ends. Then came what, in hindsight, may have been the turning point of the season. It happened at the I Love NY Open, a World Curling Tour event in the curling backwater of Utica, New York. *Gushue had Howard call the game.*

It was as much an experiment as it was an attempt to shake the team out of a funk with the Trials less than a month away. "I was fine being the fifth guy," said Howard. "Now they want me to skip the game and that was their idea. My initial thought was I'd sweep for the lead, be a second stone and when it got to Brad's shot, I'd hold the broom. But when we got to

Utica, they said, 'No, no. You're not sweeping. You're Russ Howard, the skip. So you skip.'" Gushue subsequently peeled off five straight wins in New York, including a 9-6 decision over eventual Brier champ Jean-Michel Menard of Quebec. But the foursome lost their first playoff, a 7-3 setback to Alberta's Darren Moulding. At the next bonspiel, the final event before the Trials and with Adam back at second, Team Gushue went 3-3 at Nipawin, Saskatchewan.

It was the showing in Utica, Gushue said later, that sealed the deal to insert Howard and relegate Adam to the sidelines. "We kind of saw the writing on the wall at that point," Gushue said. "Because we wanted to give ourselves the best chance at winning, we probably realized we needed Russ to be in the lineup. Everybody's confidence seemed to increase with him out there. We knew our strategy was going to be good and our line calling was going to be good with him. It just improved the team. He's a very intense guy on the ice and I have the utmost respect for that. He's out there focused and wants to win. He almost demands to win and that's one thing I love about him. He expects that from everybody else as well."

It would be the last time Adam would see any ice time of consequence, although by all accounts he was fine with the decision. Like the others on the team, Adam had started curling at an early age. He was in Grade eight in Wabush, Labrador, and playing hockey when he accompanied his parents to the curling club. "My Mom and Dad curled, so they got me over to give it a try," he recalled to the *Aurora*, a Labrador City weekly newspaper. "At first I didn't really like it, but it kind of grew on me and then I started to play competitive curling and I gave up hockey."

Adam and Nichols hooked up in 1996, with Adam playing in his first provincial championship. Their camaraderie on the ice would also form the basis of a solid friendship. With the Trials just around the corner, it would later be said that Adam stepped up and volunteered to move aside for Howard. Truth is, Adam was not offered much of a choice during a team meeting at coach McDonald's house. Just as he had been at three Briers, Adam would be Gushue's fifth man. "I think everyone knew, in the back of our mind," Adam told the St. John's *Express*, "that our most successful lineup was with Russ in there. Nobody wants to be told to sit out... but we've got to look at what's best for the team. I figured I've got no problem taking a back seat for Russ Howard because he's a phenomenal curler."

"We're all committed to winning," said Gushue at the time. "Egos aside, it's got to come down to what's working." ♣

CHAPTER 7

The men's field that was gathering at the Tim Hortons Canadian Olympic Trials in Halifax from December 3 - 11 was said to be the deepest ever assembled. Leading the pack were Randy Ferbey and Kevin Martin. Depending on who you talked to, Ferbey was the man to beat. Others felt the Trials title was Martin's to lose. Martin was the defending Olympic silver medalist, having placed second in Salt Lake City in 2002 following a loss to Pal Trulsen in the gold-medal game. Martin curled in the 1992 Albertville Games when curling was a demonstration sport, placing fourth. He also owned two Brier titles.

Ferbey, as Russ Howard alluded to, was rapidly making a strong case as the leader of the best curling team ever assembled. With Ferbey calling the game and throwing third stone while Dave Nedohin tossed last rocks, the Edmonton foursome accumulated four Brier wins and three world championships. Ferbey also won two Briers curling third for Pat Ryan in 1988 and 1989. But he didn't have much luck in his only Trials appearance, finishing 5-4 at the 2001 qualifier in Regina.

Then there was Winnipeg's Jeff Stoughton, who had two Brier titles and a world championship under his belt, and Glenn Howard, who was curling in his fourth straight Trials. After putting together his own team following his days curling third for older brother Russ, Glenn Howard had consistently been a threat on the World Curling Tour. Nova Scotians

Mark Dacey, winner of the 2004 Brier after finishing second to Ferbey in 2003, and Shawn Adams, runner-up in the 2005 Brier, were sure to be buoyed by the hometown crowd. Then you could toss a few others into the mix: Calgary's John Morris, a two-time world junior champ on the cusp of breaking through on the men's circuit with a Brier title; Pat Ryan, who despite being fifty-one still had the touch; and Jay Peachey, who slipped into the Trials following his third-place finish at the 2004 Canadian championship.

Privately, few people gave the Gushue team much of a chance. In fact,

CURLING TERMS

HAMMER

The last shot of the end.

Stoughton created a firestorm when he declared in the Winnipeg Free Press that Gushue had "no chance" of winning. The Gushue team elected to take the high road, refusing to engage in a war of words with Stoughton. Few knew it at the time, but Gushue had much more pressing matters to worry about than a few flippant remarks made to a newspaper reporter. The more important story, broken by the St. John's *Telegram*, didn't come out until a day before the Trials final, but it made headlines from coast to coast. Gushue had been playing the 2005 curling season with an aching heart. His mother, Maureen, had been diagnosed with bowel cancer in August at the age of fifty-three. In early September, she underwent surgery followed by chemotherapy which continued up to, and following, the Trials.

Brad is the only son of Maureen and Ray Gushue, who also have a daughter, Natasha. He is a boy who any Mama would love to call their own. "It's been tough," he said in Halifax. "I'm very close to my Mom." Gushue contemplated not curling, and in fact it took every ounce of

Many in the curling world were stunned when Brad Gushue added
veteran Russ Howard to the team for the Olympic Trials.

(Canadian Press photo)

strength for him to board that plane leaving for Norway in September. Of course, there was some coaxing – perhaps insistence – from his mother. "She wants me to go out and curl and to play in the spiels," he said. "She said, 'Brad, I'm fine. You go and do what you got to do and enjoy it.' It was tough and I really didn't want to go. But she wanted me to go and it's the only reason I went."

"I told him, 'Brad, you've worked so hard, you can't give up now. I won't let you,'" Maureen Gushue recounted.

Through the fall, hardly a day went by on the road that Gushue was not talking to his mother. His teammates were aware of his pain and gave him his space. At the same time, they were there to prop him up when needed. "I rarely asked him about his Mom because I knew when he was with us he didn't have to worry about people asking him how his Mom was, answering questions all the time," Nichols said. "We could only imagine what he was going through. It's your Mom, right? I'd ask him every now and again, every couple of spiels, how was everything going. And if he wanted to talk, he could talk. And if he didn't say anything, I just left it alone."

Maureen's brave fight may have been part of the reason that Brad didn't let the team's lackluster play on the Tour pre-Trials consume him. From a curling standpoint, her illness put everything in perspective. He had been starting to think that curling was more than just a sport – until Maureen got the fateful news. "When that all happened, you soon realized it was only a game. Curling became such a secondary thing, I didn't even want to play. But she didn't want to let anything happening to her affect our lives. She wanted everything to be normal and she still wants it that way."

There was no question Gushue's team entered the Trials as the underdog. Still, the 2001 Trials had proved if nothing else that a dog can have a big bite. Mike Harris had basically been a little-known curler from Ontario. But despite his status, Harris finished ahead of Martin, Stoughton, Middaugh, Russ Howard, Burtnyk, and Werenich to earn a trip to the 1998 Nagano Olympic Games. Howard recalls playing Martin in the 1997 Trials when Martin looked at him and asked, "Who's this Mike Harris guy?"

"We know if we play our average game," Gushue said before leaving for Halifax, "we're probably not going to win. But if we play the way we're capable of playing, we've beaten every team up here before and there's no reason to think we can't beat six out of nine teams in the round-robin to get in the playoffs and then win two more games. It's not as tough as people think."

Actually, there was one team Gushue hadn't bested and that was Martin. Their last meeting had been in St. John's at the Players Championship the previous spring. But Martin was limping into Nova Scotia having failed to qualify for the playoffs in Nipawin, Saskatchewan, after losing three straight games. Still, he was third on the World Curling Tour's money list with $37,000. Ferbey was on top of the money list with $56,741, and in the week before the Trials he had peeled off eight straight victories to win an event in Yorkton, Saskatchewan.

> "Brad's probably the most seasoned young curler in the world, but he's still not as seasoned as Randy Ferbey."
> - RUSS HOWARD

If Stoughton's "no chance" comments made news, so did Gushue's decision to insert Howard into the lineup at second and calling the game. It was a surprise to most of the curlers in the ten-team field – and to Howard, for that matter. "I thought I was the fifth man/coach/water boy/

cheerleader/psychologist," he joked. "Then I find out they want me to curl, which was a bit of a shock." Martin, for one, was stunned by the move. He told reporters in Alberta he felt a switch at this stage of the game – sliding a Hall of Famer just shy of fifty into a team full of twenty-somethings – would shake up the team's chemistry. But those fears, Howard said, were eased by coach McDonald who handled the situation, in Howard's words, "beautifully."

McDonald's summation was simple: the team is struggling and is it going to win the Trials the way it's playing? No. Russ Howard is sitting on the bench. Does it make sense to use him? Yes. "That reasoning calmed my fears," said Howard. "Brad's probably the most seasoned young curler in the world, but he's still not as seasoned as Randy Ferbey. Me, I'm seasoned, pickled and part put away. I certainly don't fear any of those guys like Randy Ferbey or Kevin Martin. After you've beaten all those teams, you're not in awe." ●

CHAPTER 8

Team Gushue opened the 2005 Olympic Trials on the afternoon of Saturday, December 3, against Russ Howard's younger brother, Glenn. If it's true that teams need a tough match early on to work out the butterflies, the Gushue rink found it in Glenn Howard, a seven-time Brier veteran. Glenn and Russ Howard are as close as any two brothers can be, although geography (Russ is in Moncton, New Brunswick, while Glenn resides in Penetanguishene, Ontario, where he runs a Beer Store franchise) dictates they don't see much of each other except on curling ice. So it was ironic that Russ's first game with a new team – a Newfoundland and Labrador team, at that – would be against his long-time third.

Glenn jumped out to an early 2-0 lead, but Gushue battled back to grab a 4-3 lead after five ends. Then Glenn delivered what looked to be a punishing blow with three in the sixth for a 6-4 lead. Undaunted, Gushue tied it with two in the seventh and stole two more points in the eighth for an 8-6 advantage. The final score read 9-7 for Gushue.

"What I'm really impressed with [in] these kids," said Russ Howard, "is their maturity when they fall behind. I've played with a ton of teams that couldn't come back from the three-ender we gave up. It just goes to show what these guys are made of."

Each of the teams at the Trials was assigned colours, and Newfoundland's hunter orange was drawing plenty of attention. The

Gushue team was the butt of more than a few jokes mid-week, which amused the fellow Newfoundlanders. "We went by the airport the other day," smiled Gushue, "and they wanted us to guide a few planes in." Added Howard: "I radiate."

Although they elected to keep their cards close to their chest, the Newfoundland team was upset by Stoughton's "no chance" comment, even if the other members of the Stoughton team – Jon Mead, Garry Vandenberghe, and Steve Gould – called the Gushue foursome to apologize for the skip's remarks. Howard elected to see things rationally. After the tournament, he said he hadn't blamed the Winnipeg skip for making the forecast. Besides, what had the Gushue team won at the men's level, other than the Canada Cup East event?

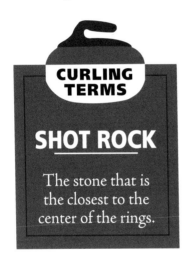

CURLING TERMS

SHOT ROCK

The stone that is the closest to the center of the rings.

Meanwhile, Gushue savoured the win for another reason. Perhaps, he said, this might silence the cynics who insisted that making Russ Howard a starter would screw up the team chemistry.

That point was hammered home Sunday when Gushue registered two wins to sit alone in first place after three draws. The big victory came Sunday night on national television with a 9-6 decision over Ferbey. Gushue had earlier in the day dispatched Adams 10-7. Ferbey trailed 7-6 with hammer in the 10th end and appeared to have it set up for at least one, but Nedohin failed to make a tough draw wide around a pair of well-positioned Gushue guards protecting a pair of rocks that were counting.

"Ridiculous," Ferbey spat as he made his way to the media interview area afterwards. The Alberta skip was upset with his front end and the

Russ Howard was surprised to learn his role with the team had been elevated from fifth man to second stone where he replaced Mike Adam. Howard held the broom for Brad Gushue's final shots.

(Canadian Press photo)

usually sure-handed Nedohin. And he certainly was not about to start heaping praise on Gushue. "I'm not worried about Gushue's play," he growled when asked about the surprising Newfoundland skip who had jumped from the gate with three straight wins. "I'm not even commenting on that. I'm worried about my team."

But there was a lot to talk about in Gushue's shot making. He curled ninety-three per cent against Ferbey, and after three games he led all skips with a sizzling ninety-two per cent efficiency rate. That excellence was evident in the sixth end against Ferbey when Gushue executed a beautiful runback (bumping up a stone) to knock out two Ferbey stones, score two, and grab a 5-4 lead. The shot drew a loud applause from the pro-Newfoundland crowd of 6,475 gathered in the Metro Centre. "The average curler," Howard said, "is never going to make that shot, and he's got it all the way down." Gushue then ran his unbeaten streak to four games with a 10-4 dismantling of Dacey the next day. But Howard reminded him there was still plenty of curling left yet. This was the voice of experience, offering caution to his younger curling partner.

Gushue and Howard actually roomed together in Halifax and while you'd think the topic of conversation between the two would have been curling 24/7, Gushue says it wasn't the case. Sure, the youngster did pick the master's brain, but Gushue was also getting on-the-job-training just having Howard wearing the same garish Halloween-orange colours. Howard was there to call the game and call line on last shot, make no mistake, yet this was still Brad Gushue's team. "I was in control, and that's because I'm a bit of a control freak, I guess," says Gushue with a smile.

Even though they had only curled together in a handful of games, Gushue and Howard already appeared to be working in sync. Sure, there were times Howard would bellow a "Hurrrrry ... harrrrrd!" with more gusto than usual, and he was not shy to wear his emotions on his sleeve, turning with disgust on a missed shot. But

> ## "I was in control, and that's because I'm a bit of a control freak, I guess."
>
> - BRAD GUSHUE

that was Howard, whose energy for the game and ferocity to win was unmatched by most half his age. Howard and Gushue appeared to be on the same page. Even if Howard called a shot Gushue didn't like, he knew enough to let the kid do his thing. "There were times Brad said, 'I can make it,' and that was enough for me," Howard said.

"The one thing I was surprised at, and it was a big confidence boost for me, was that I felt I was on the same level as Russ," Gushue said. "I felt he was gaining just as much from us as we were from him. That was the biggest thing he brought to the team. It made us realize we could win games at that level and that's a confidence boost. Once you believe, you go out and do it. The whole strategy thing was a little overstated on our team. The thing is, there weren't many calls changed. We were good enough. We just didn't believe it. That belief came from Russ."

Howard admired Gushue's demeanor. It was evident, he said, the kid was well-schooled. After the win over Ferbey, Gushue was thinking about the next game ten minutes later. Nobody had to remind him a win over Randy Ferbey in Draw three did not translate into a berth in the final. But it was clear Gushue was riding the proverbial high with a 4-0 start and making noise at the "Roar of the Rings," as the Trials were dubbed. Team Gushue was also becoming a darling of the Halifax fans. At a greasy spoon near their hotel, where the team would converge for fish cakes each day, fans would often approach the curlers for autographs and photos.

Back on the ice, Ryan, who at fifty was 144 days older than Howard, was enjoying his status as the elder statesman in the ten-team field. Ryan had won back-to-back Briers as part of the great Ryan's Express Alberta teams in 1988-89, with Ferbey curling third and Don Walchuck, Martin's vice, at second. He won the world championship in 1989. Ryan added a third Brier win and second world crown curling third for Rick Folk's British Columbia rink in 1994. The veteran skip showed Gushue he still had what it takes, knocking Newfoundland from the ranks of the unbeaten with a 9-5 loss. Perhaps Gushue could be blamed for looking ahead to a game that evening, because he curled only sixty-five per cent against Ryan.

On the schedule that December 6th evening was a clash with Stoughton. TSN was carrying it live and no doubt the whole "no chance" storyline would be played up big time. Fortunately, the curlers didn't disappoint. Gushue rebounded from a poor effort against Ryan with a brilliant game against Stoughton, and Nichols emerged as a force with an equally splendid effort.

The Newfoundlanders were actually in trouble in the seventh end, but a splendid Nichols heavy-weight runback, a hard toss that bumped up a rock and wiped out three Stoughton stones, held the Winnipeggers to a single point. In the ninth, Nichols set up some Gushue heroics with an off-in shot off a Stoughton rock to the four foot, removing Stoughton's shot rock along the way. "That's as a good as I've seen him play in a long time," Gushue later said of his third. "He's played games where he's been ninety-five per cent, but the degree of difficulty he had today and some of the shots we called for that he made were spectacular. He was the MVP."

But Gushue arguably made the shot of the Trials in the ninth end: a spectacular double to count four after trailing 4-3. Holding last shot, Gushue was counting one in the ninth with two Stoughton rocks also nestled in the four foot. Rather than opt for the single takeout and two points, Gushue elected for the trickier double which he made perfectly. "Russ wasn't sure it was there and he was leaning towards the softer weight for two. But I could see myself making it and seeing the rocks flying out and getting four or five," Gushue said. "I would have been regretting it if I didn't play it. It was my best shot this week. I threw it very well and Russ did a great job calling line. I wanted to sweep it and he called the sweepers off. I just hit it perfect and both of the rocks flew out. It was a nice feeling."

Gushue didn't know it, but his most ardent fan, his mother, was not in the stands to see the shot live. She was back at the hotel watching on TV after leaving during the fifth-end break because she hadn't been feeling well. "That really hurt," he said afterwards. "When I found out she had to leave, I didn't have a lot of joy about the win. My whole concern was for her at that point."

Gushue and John Morris were both 5-1 after six draws, with Ryan, Stoughton, and Kevin Martin close behind at 4-2. The story of the Trials so far, outside of Gushue's game, had been the play of Ferbey's team. The foursome had slipped to 2-4 and were likely out of contention. The home teams, Dacey at 1-5 and Adams at 2-4, were not faring any better. Ferbey later acknowledged that four years of Olympic preparation had gone down the tubes. "We just didn't perform here [in Halifax]," he said. As the playoffs drew closer, Gushue flirted with disaster at mid-week, but managed to squeak out a 7-6 decision over Jay Peachey, his nemesis from the 2004 Brier, who entered the game winless in six starts.

The teams were even at 6-6 through nine ends, thanks in part to a pair of blown opportunities by Gushue in the eighth and ninth ends. He had a perfect chance to ice Peachey in the eighth with a hit and stick for three, but his shooter rolled out taking with it Gushue's second counter meaning he had to settle for one. In the ninth, Gushue's last shot sailed through the house and Peachey picked up a deuce. Gushue had last shot in the 10th and Peachey was poised for a steal of one in the final end with a pair of rocks harbored in the four foot, protected by a centerline guard. To throw a shot heavy enough to oust the pair of Peachey rocks, Gushue would have to go through the guard. Then, just as he'd done all week, Gushue calmly stepped into the hack and released a perfect draw to the left side of the ice as sweepers Korab and Nichols carried the rock deftly to the pin. Gushue would say afterwards it was the toughest draw he'd ever have to make in order to win a game. "The cardiac kids," grinned Howard, "and it's me who's going to have the coronary."

The media, especially the scribes from Western Canada, were finally beginning to take notice of the 6-1 team. The stereotypical questions about Newfoundlanders partying on George Street (the bar and restaurant district of downtown St. John's) in celebration of the curling team's play – any team's play, for that matter, or any political or cultural gain – were pointed at Gushue ad nauseam. "Why not?" he answered when asked if his team was looking at the curling upset of the ages. "Someone's got to win and why can't it be us?" Even at 6-1 and with two draws remaining, Gushue was still not guaranteed a playoff berth, although a split of their

Brad Gushue moves one step closer to his Olympic dream.

(Canadian Press photo)

final two games on Thursday would guarantee them at least a tie-breaker. And the schedule, wouldn't you know it, saved the best for last.

On deck was Martin, who was teetering on elimination at 4-3 and Morris, who shared top spot with Gushue at 6-1. Gushue chose the right time to snap his winless streak against Martin, scoring an 8-7 win over the reigning Olympic silver medalist in the morning. Leading 8-4 after eight ends, Gushue made things interesting in the ninth with a missed double, opening the gates for Martin to score three. In the final end, Martin's last rock picked up a piece of debris – a bit of dust or perhaps a piece of fabric from the curling brooms – setting up an open double for the win. (The term "pick" includes any tiny piece of debris or even a footprint that affects the path of the rocks. This complaint would be voiced frequently later in Italy.)

It was another disappointing last rock loss of Olympic proportions for the Edmonton skip. In Salt Lake City, Martin's last shot slid a few inches too far giving Norway's Trulsen the gold. In Halifax, the Martin team could only reflect on what could have been, and Bartlett, the Newfoundland-born lead, wondered aloud if it was all worth it, admitting his hectic curling schedule had cost him his marriage. "My wife is one of the nicest people I've ever met," he said as his eyes welled with tears. "She never gave me grief. I knew she didn't like it. Nobody would like it when your husband is away almost half the year. You raise the kids by yourself. It's just too much time away."

Looking on from above in a Metro Centre luxury suite, Jack MacDuff could only marvel at Gushue's game. While Newfoundland's only Brier winner was convinced good things lay ahead for Gushue, MacDuff was not certain they would come this soon. With Gushue's obsession to practice, practice, and practice some more, MacDuff said, Gushue reminded him of a golfer with the same characteristics – Eldrick "Tiger" Woods. "Not a lot of people have that drive," MacDuff said.

With Morris losing 8-6 to Howard in the morning draw, all that separated Gushue and a direct trip to Sunday's final was a win over Morris, the Calgarian-via-Ottawa, in the evening. It wasn't even close. Morris shot just sixty-one per cent as Gushue won 7-4 in nine ends to finish the round-robin alone in first place at 8-1. Fans started to wonder if Howard was destined to celebrate his milestone fiftieth birthday in Turin, Italy, on the 19th of February, the day Canada was scheduled to play New Zealand in the 20th Winter Olympic Games.

But first Gushue and the rest of the team had to figure out what to do for two days. He would later say the idle time was the biggest hurdle he had to clear all week, that he was frightfully nervous – or "shitbaked" – for

After winning the Olympic Trials, Brad Gushue made a dash for the stands and a family hug with his father, Ray, mother, Maureen, and his fiancée, Krista Tibbo. *(Canadian Press photo)*

forty-eight straight hours. Meanwhile, Morris's slide continued that Friday evening with an 8-6 semifinal loss to Stoughton, setting the stage for the "no chance" rematch.

On the morning of the Sunday championship, Winnipeg Free Press curling writer Paul Wiecek perhaps summed up the feelings of many Westerners when he penned a column with a particularly snotty tone: "It was suggested on press row here last week that the key to a Jeff Stoughton victory against Newfoundland's Brad Gushue in the men's final of the Canadian Curling Trials today could be as simple as Stoughton bringing a common cosmetic accessory to the game – a mirror."

And in case his point wasn't clear, he went on to elaborate. "Hold it up to Gushue's face, the thinking goes, and Stoughton might achieve two major victories before the game even started. First, it would serve to remind Gushue, who's been red-hot all week and having the bonspiel of his life, that he is still just Gushue, a twenty-five-year-old relative curling neophyte who has a world junior curling championship on his resume but nothing of consequence since he graduated to the men's game."

Then he aimed an even lower blow at the team from the Rock. "And second, it would also serve to remind Gushue that he's from Newfoundland, a relative curling backwater that has won only one Canadian men's curling championship in the history of the Brier – and none for exactly thirty years. Remind Gushue who he is and where he's from, in other words, and Stoughton could plant the seeds of self-doubt just as the young skip is about to curl the biggest game of his life," Wiecek penned.

Gushue wasn't aware of the column, but such cynicism was not uncommon. "This year we've been put down more than any other year, just little comments you hear and all the Internet stuff," Gushue said. "So we just decided to put ourselves in a shell and, really, when it comes down to it, there's only six people that matter. You have to believe you can win and those six people do believe it."

"Someone's got to win and why can't it be us?"

- BRAD GUSHUE

A crowd of 8,450 spun the turnstiles at the Metro Centre on a chilly December 11 afternoon, bringing the total attendance for the week to 159,235, a new Olympic Curling Trials record. It was easy to tell who the Nova Scotians were rooting for at the event: many came wearing the hunter orange that Gushue's team had made so popular. A few improvised and donned orange garbage bags. Many others held signs jeering Stoughton for his "no chance" remark. On this Sunday afternoon, there would be no references to Gushue being the "Broken Man on a Halifax

Pier," to quote the famous Stan Rogers ballad "Barrett's Privateers." Instead, the curler whom Stoughton had dismissed got the Winnipeg skip in the crosshairs.

Gushue dominated early on, grabbing a 6-2 lead after four ends, but Stoughton whittled away at the lead and it came down to the final end (doesn't it always?) with Gushue clinging to an 8-6 lead and Stoughton holding the hammer. Then Nichols missed on a peel on his last shot to leave a Stoughton corner guard, and overtime – or perhaps even a Stoughton come-from-behind win – suddenly loomed, especially after Manitoba third Jon Mead buried a rock on his last shot.

Stoughton tried a hit-and-roll on his first rock to sit two behind the corner guard, but the shot failed to curl and just rolled outside the rings. Mead would later blame himself for failing to call off the sweepers. Gushue played a raise takeout to remove Stoughton's shot rock, and after the Manitoban drew to the house on his last shot, a measurement verified that Stoughton's first stone was outside the rings, if only by a hair. "Lard tunderin' Jesus," Howard exclaimed in his best Newfoundland accent. "It feels awesome, I'll tell ya. I could swim to Italy." So much for the chemistry knock. Howard's move had become, as some suggested, the "Shrewd of Turin."

Afterwards, Stoughton gave full marks to the Gushue team, although he refused to retract his earlier controversial statements. "I said what I said because that's what I felt at the time," said Stoughton in standup fashion. "I've been proven wrong and that's fine. It's not the first time I've been proven wrong." As for Gushue, following a group hug with his teammates, he raced to the sidelines where his mother and fianceé, Krista Tibbo, waited.

"It means a lot having her here to see this," he said of his mother. "It has been tough, and obviously for her, too. She's been my biggest fan, and her biggest concern was being here this week to support me. The fact she put my curling career that far above herself, I guess that's what mothers do. My thoughts were with her all week and I'm just glad we won and I think it's going to make her real happy. It's special."

"I'm so proud," a teary-eyed Maureen Gushue said as her son and his mates were handed their medals. "When I was diagnosed with cancer, he basically said he'd rather be with me, but I told him he had to go follow his dream. When I had surgery, he stayed by my side. He was there the whole week I was in hospital. He's been really supportive towards me and I've been supportive towards him."

Until Gushue, Nichols, Korab, and Adam came along, only one born-and-raised Newfoundlander – hockey player Dwayne Norris, who skated in the 1994 Lillehammer Games – had ever competed in the Winter Olympics. Now, in addition to a trip to Italy, the team also qualified for Sport Canada funding, which amounted to $174,000 tax free dollars over two and a half years. That money looked pretty good. Nichols had just graduated from Memorial University with a kinesiology degree. Adam was still in school. And Gushue (another MUN grad) had quit his job as an insurance salesman the previous summer when his former boss posed an ultimatum: choose either curling or insurance. At this point, Gushue knew he'd made the right decision. 🥌

CHAPTER 9

Except for the few wrinkles on Russ Howard's face, the curlers on Brad Gushue's team were beginning to look pretty young and hip. And they were also a hot commodity. They were feted at dinners at their home curling club, invited to Government House to dine with the Lieutenant Governor and the Premier, and honoured at the St. John's Athlete of the Year banquet when Gushue was named the city's top jock for 2005.

Life was now dramatically different for the Olympic-bound curling team. On his way to dinner with the Queen's representative in Newfoundland, Gushue had one fervent fan walk up to his car at a red light and knock on the window offering a handshake.

"All of a sudden you're a star. It's different, definitely different. You almost want to find a way to get back to what you were used to for twenty-five years. But don't get me wrong, it's all been very nice," he said at the time, albeit with a bit of hesitation. "A half-hour trip to the mall turns into two hours and you hear people saying your name and you see people staring. It kind of makes me a little paranoid, actually," he said.

Four young Newfoundlanders now had a province collectively feeling good about itself, even if some scribes from other parts of Canada were taking cheap shots after the big win. The mood was certainly dampened by a column from the Toronto Sun's Bill Lankhof, who wrote that the win was the "biggest thing to happen in The Land Cod Forgot since the

It was a different greeting Jeff Thomas had for Brad Gushue at St. John's International Airport in December, 2005 after Gushue won the Olympic Trials. Thomas was at the airport in 2000 to console the curler after he lost the Canadian junior final.

(Don Power/The Express photo)

invention of the pogey cheque. Newfies finally have someone named Skip to look up to again whose livelihood doesn't depend on a cod fish to be born later.

Locals now have something to chew the fat over – other than that yucky whale blubber they've been gnawing on for those CBC retrospectives the past fifty years." Satire, in this instance, had crossed the line to insult, and Newfoundlanders flooded Lankhof with heated emails and phone calls.

Gushue, of course, was not paying much attention to all the shenanigans. He was busy looking ahead to Italy and the Olympics which were just under two months away. Nobody had to tell him Canada entered the Games as a favourite, even though the country was still seeking its first men's gold medal. Everyone was trying to focus on training. Over the course of the next few weeks, Howard would join the team in St. John's for practice sessions. In one case, Paul Webster, the Canadian Curling Association's assistant national development coach, flew to the city and, for whatever reason, tried to make his mark on the team. "I fly over there to throw rocks with the guys a month before the Olympics," Howard recalls, "and this guy's [Webster] out there with a video camera trying to change their delivery. I put a stop to that in a hurry."

The Gushue team had a record of 14-2 with Howard in the lineup, starting with the Utica, New York, spiel and continuing through the Trials. But almost three weeks had passed since the Halifax win and the curlers were anxious to play a game for real.

Their first competition since the Trials was the BDO Classic Canadian Open, a Grand Slam event in Winnipeg that would include many of the teams in the Trials along with Pal Trulsen and the United States Olympic representative, Pete Fenson. The Canadian Open offered up $100,000 in prize money, but Gushue was not distracted. His focus was not on Winnipeg, but Turin. Everything else was just a stepping stone. "I guess you could say this is a glorified training session," he said of the Open.

After Winnipeg, Gushue and Co. had another event on the calendar, the Strauss Canada Cup in Kamloops. The team got a free pass to the B.C. interior as a result of its Trials victory. If Gushue, Nichols, Howard, Korab, and Adam were feeling good about their win at the Trials, the mood might have been quelled with only a pair of wins each in Winnipeg

When you're a champion, you get to ride in fancy limos, like this one that ferried the Gushue team to a reception at John's Curling Club after it arrived home from the Olympic Trials. *(Joe Gibbons/The Telegram photo)*

and Kamloops. Even in their own backyard, Newfoundlanders were whispering the "F" word. Was Gushue's win in Halifax, dare we say it, a fluke? Would Canada's stretch of gold-less Olympic Games stretch to three in a row? Even though ninety-four per cent of the world's curlers, according to the World Curling Federation, live in North America's Great White North?

Relax, said Kevin Martin, pointing out the obvious talent in Nichols and Gushue, coupled with Howard's experience. "You've got people there who shoot high percentages," said the reigning Olympic silver medalist. "I like our chances. No question we have the horses to win two gold medals [in hockey and curling]."

Following the Strauss Canada Cup in British Columbia, the Gushue team jetted east with a stopover in Toronto. From there, they headed for Europe, first to Paris and then into Turin via Milan. Despite the marginal play in Western Canada, Gushue had plenty of confidence packed away in his suitcase. "We don't have the pedigree of a Randy Ferbey or a Kevin Martin," he said, "but we know we're a good team, and if we go in and play like we did in Halifax, our chances are as good as anybody's."

Perhaps McDonald summed it up in layman's terms. "I was talking to a good friend, Ralph O'Brien [the owner/entertainer of a well-known St. John's Irish watering hole] down at Erin's Pub one day and he asked how I felt we'll do," recalls the coach. "I said, 'Ralph, it's a little bit like you getting up on stage and playing your five best songs. How do you think you'll do?' He said, 'I'll do well.' Well, that's how I expect the boys to do. That's their stage. That's the way it is. They're really good. I don't expect they will have an absolute abysmal game. Even on a bad day, Wayne Gretzky was good. On our worst day, I still think we should be competitive with everybody."

If the field in Halifax was the best ever assembled, Turin wasn't far off. Peja Lindholm was a three-time world champion and had represented Sweden in the 1998 and 2002 Olympics, finishing fourth in Salt Lake

City. Pal Trulsen was the defending champion and, in many people's eyes, the best pure shooter in the Games. He had skipped in eight world championships, winning a silver and two bronze medals. Ralph Stoeckli, the Ferrari-driving Swiss skip, placed second in the 2003 worlds and was the 1997 world junior champion. Finland was skipped by Markku Uusipaavalniemi (M-15, for the fifteen letters in his last name), who had placed no worst than fifth in the worlds since 2000. He was one of the best shooters in the field and might have won a world championship if he was surrounded by a stronger supporting cast.

   The rest of the list was just as impressive. Great Britain's David Murdoch was the reigning world championship silver medalist and 2003

CURLING TERMS

END

Curling's version of a period or inning.

European champion, and Andy Kapp of Germany appeared in eight world championships, winning silver in 1997. He also curled at the Nagano and Salt Lake City Olympics. Sheep farmer Sean Becker of New Zealand and Joel Retornaz of Italy rounded out the field. Retornaz got a free pass to the Olympics as the host team.

   Team Gushue arrived four days prior to the opening ceremonies, and six days before their first game, in order to soak up the atmosphere of the Olympic Games. Gushue admitted he was a little awestruck his first day in the Village, recognizing familiar faces such as hockey stars Hayley Wickenheiser and Cassie Campbell and speed skater Clara Hughes. The Village was a series of residences spread over twenty-four acres, housing upwards of 2,500 athletes from eighty-five participating nations. It had all the amenities of home, with two restaurants, a shopping centre and a gym. Located in the southern part of Turin, it was close to the Main Media Centre constructed to accommodate the 10,000 print and electronic journalists covering the Games. The Main Media Centre was located in an area known as the Lingotto and housed in the former Fiat plant, a building that had autos whipping around its rooftop in the 1969 Michael Caine film "The Italian Job."

Though quaint and charming in the old city with its venerable architecture, Turin is very much an industrial town. Like Detroit, another metropolis built on autos that had also staged a large sporting event (the 2006 Super Bowl), it was falling on hard times. One of the biggest crises was that Fiat, which had controlled the local economy, went into an economic tailspin in 2002, cutting as many as 8,000 jobs. Turin is still trying to recover from the blow.

To the locals, the city is known as Torino, the same as Roma or Milano. To the English-speaking world, it's officially known as Turin, with a population of just under a million people and at one time the capital of Italy. With a price-tag of $15 billion for the 2006 Games, quaint towns such as Lake Placid or Albertville or Lillehammer can no longer afford to stage the event. Turin's record as the biggest city to play host to the Olympics will be short-lived, however, with Vancouver on the horizon in 2010.

When Russ Howard arrived in Italy, he soon learned that while he was a household name in many parts of Canada, he was "Russ who?" in Turin. On the day after the team landed, the Canadian Olympic Committee called a news conference to introduce Canada's rock slingers to the world press corps. Howard, however, left his credentials at the Village. Armed (police) Polizia, and the Carabinieri (a military police) refused to let the Canadian through the heavily-secured athletes and media area. "I've never worn accreditation in my entire life," said Howard with a grin, after someone from the Canadian delegation hustled back to the village to retrieve his ID. "At every Brier or Olympic Trials or Grand Slam or whatever, everybody knew me. So I always threw it in the garbage on the first day and away I went."

Howard had been considered as a candidate to carry Canada's flag in the opening ceremonies, thanks largely in part to a campaign started in his adopted hometown of Moncton. Some high-profile athletes such as cross-country skier Beckie Scott, bobsledder Pierre Lueders, and speed skaters Cindy Klassen and Clara Hughes said they would prefer not to carry the flag, mainly because of the short turnaround time between the opening ceremonies and their competition. But Howard said he would jump at the chance. Alas, he finished runner-up to female hockey veteran Danielle Goyette in the voting to select a flag-bearer.

The opening was a glittery, fiery spectacle with a smattering of the glamorous and the famous, from Sophia Loren, stunning as ever, to Luciano Pavarotti and three-time Olympic gold-medalist and Italian skiing darling Alberto Tomba. Presidential and prime ministerial spouses Laura Bush and Cherie Blair were also on hand, the latter holding up traffic for miles on Turin's freeways as her car sped along with a police escort to Stadio Olimpico.

The stadium was originally erected in the 1930s under dictator Benito Mussolini, but it had been spiffed up to the tune of millions for the twentieth Games. Pop music from the '70s and '80s disco era, together with the cheers of 35,000, greeted the athletes as they entered the stadium. One of the loudest ovations was reserved for Canada. "Just before we walked into the opening," recalled Nichols, "we were all lined up ready to march in and Danielle Goyette grabbed the Canadian flag and started waving it and all the Canadians just went crazy. That was the first time I went, 'Oh my God, I'm at the Olympic Games!' That was even more [dramatic] than when we checked into the Village. The Village was cool because you're with the best athletes in the world. But the opening

Torino bound: Brad Gushue, Mark Nichols, Russ Howard, Jamie Korab, Mike Adam and Toby McDonald. *(Joe Gibbons/The Telegram photo)*

ceremonies was the big thing. That was the first real moment that this is for real."

Gushue had similar feelings about the opening ceremonies. "I'm not sure if my feet touched the ground the whole night." In order to maintain some sense of reality, the curlers subsequently were moved away from some of the hype and hysteria. The day after the Olympic kick-off, Team Gushue shifted their camp to Pinerolo, a hamlet of about 35,000 nestled at the foot of the Alps and about forty minutes west of Turin. While Turin was the host city of the Games, the majority of the events were housed in the mountain villages of Bardonecchia, Cesana, Sestriere, Pragelato, and Sauze d'Oulx in the French-Italian Alps. Only speed skating, hockey, and figure skating were actually staged in Turin.

The Palaghiaccio is made up of two facilities, one indoors and one outdoors. The indoor facility seats 2,011, and was constructed especially for the Games — intended to be used as a hockey and curling rink post-Olympics. It offered a stark contrast to the otherwise ancient Pinerolo city centre and its pastel-coloured dwellings on winding cobblestone streets so narrow that pedestrians have to almost step into the shops to avoid passing autos. In the centre of town, tourists marveled at La Cattedrale Di San Donato, dating back to the year 1000. The curling team's digs, however, were a little more modern: the top level of a sixteen-floor apartment building, the highest in Pinerolo, complete with a breathtaking view of the Alps.

"We had four days in the village and it was a fun atmosphere to be in," Gushue recalls, "but it can get pretty frustrating because it takes so long to get in and out through security. We came home one night and they checked our accreditation six times before we even got into the village. It took us about forty-five minutes, which was very frustrating. Then you have the same food day after day. It's not a situation I'd want to be in for three weeks."

The curlers had their penthouse apartment with the great view waiting for them in Pinerolo. Their families, who were en route to Italy, also had accommodations arranged. But their move into a home away from home would not go as smoothly. Each of the players' families made the costly trip to Turin. Wendy Howard was there with the couple's two children, Stephen and Ashley. As it happens, fifteen-year-old Ashley Howard had just gotten back from Thunder Bay, Ontario, where she represented New Brunswick in the national junior women's championship. Toby McDonald had brought along his wife, Shelly, and their two children, Sarah and Mark. The parents of each of the other curlers were also in Italy. But there was one person missing.

Maureen Gushue was not well enough to make the trip. "If anything happened over here," Brad Gushue said on the eve of his Olympic debut, "it's not the place you want her to be. You want her to be home." Not that Brad would be alone in Italy. His dad was making the trip along with his fiancée. And he took comfort in the fact his mother would be in good hands back in the Southlands section of St. John's with the rest of the family. Brad's sister, Natasha, was home and Maureen's sister was travelling back to Newfoundland from Ontario. As Gushue explained to the St. John's Telegram, "I'm glad she's home, but in a selfish manner I wish she was here to be with me for a hug after the games."

Maureen Gushue had continued to undergo the chemo treatments following the Halifax Trials, and Brad felt the January medications had been particularly taxing on his mother. "Her health, frankly, is far more important than any game or any Olympics," he said at the time. "This is all so minor compared to her, and my priority is making sure she's healthy, and if it was going to sacrifice anything coming over here, there's no sense doing it."

While the team was settled into their high-rise digs, many of the family members were not so lucky. They were booked through the Canadian Curling Association into the San Secondo Hotel, in a village of the same name three kilometers from the Pinerolo town centre. Upon arriving, the McDonalds learned their rooms had been unceremoniously given to members of the Russian hockey team, which had arrived in Italy early to get in some pre-Olympic practice. This despite the fact that upwards of $15,000 had been pre-paid for accommodations. Wendy, Stephen, and Ashley Howard were in the same boat. Both families were subsequently lodged in apartments until the issue could be resolved.

The Howard family eventually returned to the San Secondo, through much lobbying by Wendy Howard, but the McDonalds never spent a single night in the hotel room for which they had paid in advance. They did, however, end up in an apartment the CCA had reserved in the event of an emergency. For the others who managed to retain their rooms at San Secondo, they were galled to learn the normal room rate was far below the $230 per night they were each paying. As the curlers' families tried to sort out their lodging issues, Toby McDonald convened a meeting with CCA officials. Under no circumstance, he ordered, were the curlers to learn about the hotel screw-ups. And they never did, until the Olympics had officially concluded.

If that wasn't enough, the families were outraged to learn that the curling tickets for which they had also pre-paid were being sold at the Palaghiaccio for a much lower price. Tickets for the round-robin portion of the curling schedule were selling for forty and twenty Euro. The semifinal and bonze-medal tickets were going for sixty and thirty Euro, while tickets for the gold-medal game were selling for seventy and forty Euro. But the families had, in most cases, paid double the face value. "The whole thing was brutal, just brutal," said Russ Howard. "There was no support there for the families. We spent $2,400 on tickets for my family just to watch me curl, which doesn't make any sense. I can't imagine Janet Gretzky paying money. Not that I'm Wayne Gretzky, but all I know is he's in the Olympics, I'm in the Olympics, and I just don't understand why our association can't make some of that stuff work."

Howard had worked himself into a real lather. "You go to the Brier and the wives are free, they have their own transportation. Here we are representing our country at the Olympic Winter Games and our families are rushing off in the ninth end to walk a couple of miles in the rain to catch a taxi that doesn't run anymore to get to a town that isn't even where the curling is being held. But all the CCA brass was over there, the president, the vice-president, the dish-washer. Paul Webster – I don't know what his capacity was – he was running around in a rented vehicle and my wife's walking with my family and Toby's family. One night, I was told Mark's family, Jamie's family, and I think Mike's family got stranded in Pinerolo and had to walk almost an hour in the rain to San Secondo. What the hell is that about?"

Gerry Peckham, the CCA's director of high performance and who was in Pinerolo, maintains the CCA did not pocket any additional money on ticket markup. He laid blame on the ticket agent through whom the CCA was dealing for providing what he termed a "faulty" information sheet. In fact, Peckham said, the CCA was not aware of the discrepancy until each family had tickets in hand. "All of a sudden we had people who had paid the equivalent of forty Euro for a ticket they were holding in their hand that was selling for twenty Euro at the gate. We were able to provide each and every member of that contingent who had been over-assessed a ticket price a reimbursement subsequent to arriving back in Canada."

As for the hotels, Peckham suggests it is all a part of doing business ... the Olympic way. The Turin Olympic Committee – TOROC – secured most of the accommodations in and around each Olympic venue during the Games. After negotiating a room charge with the Innkeeper, TOROC then released the rooms to ticket and travel agents. "TOROC takes a markup, the agents who are in business take a markup, and that's all passed along to the families. So the room that may have rented for sixty or seventy Euro pre-Olympics might well rent for 150 or 170 Euro during the Olympics. We shopped really hard for accommodations, as we did for tickets," explained Peckham. "We could have paid way more for tickets and accommodations than we wound up paying. But at the same time, you can't take a chance when you're sending twenty-odd families over that they're going to arrive and secure their own accommodations and tickets. You have to pre-purchase. So there's probably going to be at least a 100 per cent markup between the November 2005 rate and the February 2006 rate."

While all of these difficulties were being sorted out, there was tension elsewhere. Team Gushue was about to make its Winter Olympics debut. ♟

CHAPTER 10

On the evening of Monday, February 13, Gushue and his team hit the ice against Germany's Andy Kapp. It was the same day that one of Canada's medal contenders, speed-skater Jeremy Wotherspoon, finished a disappointing ninth in the 500 meters. Gushue, Nichols, Howard, and Korab doubled Kapp 10-5. But it didn't come without an eyebrow-raiser early on when Gushue missed a double in the first end, resulting in a steal of two for Kapp.

Considering the team was coming off poor showings at home in the Canadian Open and Canada Cup, skeptics from St. John's to Victoria who were watching TSN might have been whispering, 'I told you so.' "Instead of us scoring one or two," said Howard of the first end, "they steal two and you're thinking, 'Wow, how are the boys going to bounce back from that?' This is my third worlds, but you're thinking, 'Can Brad handle that?' He answered that quite nicely by making the rest of his shots." Gushue responded with two in the second, and after Kapp regained the two-point lead with a deuce in the third end, Gushue took the lead for good in the fourth end with three points.

Prior to the Olympic opener, Howard was miffed at the rocks that had been selected for the Games. Having dabbled as an icemaker, he initially found the Palaghiaccio ice sheet "beautiful," but the rocks were not curling as much as the stones used in Canada. And for a team that

Everything went so smoothly at the Trials in Halifax. But tension and frustration was setting in early on at the Olympic Games in Italy. The pressure, at times, showed on the players' faces and in their actions.
(Canadian Press photo)

liked to put a lot of rocks in play, it could create problems. Meanwhile, Gushue found fault with the ice against Germany. His last shot in the first end, the missed double, came as a result of a straight spot in the ice which caused the rock to straighten out rather than curl. There would be plenty more complaining about the rocks and ice as the competition wore on, with Howard especially griping about what might be best described as "substandard" Olympic conditions.

There were two turning points at the 20th Winter Olympics for Canada's men's curling team: the first came very early, following a loss to Sweden. The second occurred later in the schedule when Gushue dropped a game to the host team.

ON THIS DAY IN HISTORY
February 24, 2006

● Czech Republic's Katerina Neumannova winds gold in the Women's 30K individual cross-country ski race at the 20th Winter Olympics.

● A flight from St. John's, NL, to New York, NY, cost $245 on Canjet.

● The European Union opened an indepth antitrust probe into Canadian mining company Inco Ltd's $12.5 billion Cdn purchase of Falconbridge Ltd.

● In Chittagong, Bangladesh, a fire at a textile factory kills 54 people.

● Nova Scotia's Rodney MacDonald is sworn in as Canada's youngest premier.

● Philippine President Gloria Macapagal-Arroyo declares Proclamation 1017 placing the country in a state of emergency in attempt to subdue a possible military coup.

● Don Knotts, American actor, dies at the age of 82.

● John Martin, Canadian broadcaster, dies at the age of 59.

● Australian Member of Parliament and Treasurer Peter Costello challenges Muslim leaders to pledge their allegiance to Australia.

● NASA announces the unusual gamma ray burst GRB 060218 that is not yet explained may be a predecessor to a supernova. It was located 440 million light years away and lasted for 33 minutes, closer and longer than any previous gamma ray burst.

● iTunes announces it reached 1 billion song downloads. The billionth song was Coldplay's *Speed of Sound*.

● Top Five Fiction Titles of that week:
The Broker, John Grisham
Red Lily, Nora Roberts
Angels and Demons, Dan Brown
The Da Vinci Code, Dan Brown
Whiteout, Ken Follett

● The best at the box office:
Tyler Perry's *Madea's Family Reunion* grossing $30,030,661.

Sources:
www.salesdata.ca
www.thetelegram.com
www.wikipedia.com

To those rating the Olympic men's curling field, Peja Lindholm of Sweden was a very solid pick to grab a playoff spot and perhaps go all the way to the gold medal game. He once played soccer but was now a full-time curler through the winter months, and he had been to the 2002 Salt Lake City Games and the Nagano Olympics in 1998. Although he fell short of the medals both times (he lost the bronze-medal game to Switzerland in 2002), the pony-tailed Lindholm was a three-time world champion, including the 2004 worlds in Lausanne, Switzerland.

Gushue was a career 3-0 against Lindholm and should have made it 4-0 in Pinerolo. But Lady Luck tossed Gushue a brick with an 8-7 extra end loss, a game that should not have seen overtime except that Team Canada muffed shots in the seventh and tenth ends. In the tenth and up two after scoring three points in the ninth, Gushue missed an easy peel with his last shot, leaving Lindholm a simple draw for the game-tying deuce. The Swedes had three stones counting in the extra end, but both of Gushue's last two shots appeared to have picked. Gushue's first shot was supposed to be a peel, but was a nose hit that left the shooter hanging around. His final stone, which needed a piece of the button, came up short and nudged off a Lindholm stone in the four foot dropping Canada to 1-1.

Afterwards, both Gushue and Howard complained about the ice (the crew responsible was headed by Sweden's Leif Oehman). They also worried there was dust falling from the ceiling, and Gushue suggested the European teams were wearing substandard shoe grippers that left marks on the ice. Howard, especially, was surly after curling only sixty-seven per cent. It was the first sign of trouble in curling paradise. Howard and Gushue barely spoke as Howard stomped around the Palaghiaccio ice through eleven ends. After being together for two weeks before the Olympic competition had even started, cabin fever was setting in. Maybe the curlers, who were supposed to have this great chemistry, were starting to grate on each other.

With Russ Howard tossing second stones and holding the broom on Brad Gushue's last two shots, Gushue was busy sweeping for Jamie Korab and Mark Nichols while also calling the game. *(Canadian Press photo)*

Later that evening, when the team retreated to their sixteenth-floor apartment, Gushue convened a sit-down in the main living room. The air needed to be cleared. "Russ was being a little hard to deal with early in the week," Gushue now says in hindsight. "He was sick and kind of cranky and really wasn't doing a lot of things good for the team, especially during the Lindholm game. They [Sweden] could get in spots we couldn't get to and Russ was complaining about that. Something needed to be said."

The person who stepped up and laid it on the line was none other than Nichols, the usually reserved one. "It was very frustrating," said Nichols. "There was complaining about rocks, complaining about the ice and everything like that. For myself, I didn't enjoy it. You only had a certain amount of time to find a set of rocks and then you say, 'Okay, those are good.' And the next thing you know, 'No, they're not good.' If something went wrong, it wasn't because of the way you were playing, it was the rock. It was about making up excuses. Our main goal every time at practice was to make sure we got Brad two rocks that were good. Usually it was then [our job to] find me the next two best rocks. But after Brad had his rocks, it was about making sure Russ was happy, too. Because if he didn't have good rocks, it was a bit more tricky. [Then] he was complaining about the rocks."

Clearly there was a lot of tension that needed to be released. "We were killing ourselves," said Nichols. "It just wasn't the same relaxed atmosphere we had in Halifax. The reason I said what I did was maybe because I am quiet. Maybe it would have more of an effect and someone will take it seriously. It seemed like the right time to say, 'Listen guys, we need to smarten up, forget about the rocks and the ice and all that stuff and change our attitudes or we're going home with nothin'.'"

Gushue would say afterwards he'd never been any prouder of Nichols than at that moment. Howard was old school who wore his emotions on his sleeve. The Gushue team was new age, with their psychologists and massage therapists and the like. One was nearly fifty and the others were in their mid-twenties. Howard's game was intensity; the others were calm, cool, and collected, at least on the outside. "When I get intense," said Howard, "it doesn't affect my game. If anything, I think it gets the old arteries actually going. But it maybe sends the wrong message to the boys. And they're not used to it, right?"

For the first time, there appeared to be a clash of personalities and the timing could not have been worse. "It wasn't that we weren't talking, I just didn't know what to say to him," Gushue said of Howard. "I didn't know how to deal with it. When you play with someone long enough you know what to say. If Mark got upset, I knew exactly what to say to make me feel better and make him feel better. With Russ, I had no idea. I'd only been with Russ for three months and I had no idea what to do. A lot of people don't realize but they say he's so experienced," Gushue continued. "Russ had never been to an Olympics before. It was totally different than anything I'd played in before and I've been in everything Russ had been in, although Russ was there ten times more. We were rookies and he was a rookie. We all had to deal with it in different ways and not having played with him so much, we hadn't seen this side before. It was something new, but Mark stepped up into a role, into something I've always wanted him to do, to be that leader."

In his defense, Howard claims to have been battling a severe flu just prior to and during the first couple of days of the Olympics. Why the team traveled all the way to Kamloops prior to the Games, he said, was, "beyond me. We're running around and running around and I showed up in Italy with one of the worst colds I've ever had. I was a mess." Coupled with his medical woes, Howard was upset with the attitude the Canadian Curling Association took towards the rocks that were slated to be used in Pinerolo. "Everybody and their uncle knew they were terrible rocks. I knew that the day after we won in Halifax."

Unfortunately, the problem didn't get fixed. "I called Shorty Jenkins," says Howard, "and he said the rocks are going to be dead straight. This was in November. Our association just sits back and goes, 'Whatever. Deal with it.' I don't think our association should represent us that way. It's the Olympic Games and it's awfully important for our country to win a medal. We should be in there fighting for the proper conditions."

It reached a boiling point against Sweden when Howard curled horribly. "So I was pretty upset with myself and the whole situation and the kids had never seen that before. They're used to the psychologists and, you know, smile-all-the-time attitude. I'm kind of an old warrior and if I'm upset, I'll be upset and it's not going to affect the game. We sit down for this meeting, it was like, 'Geez Russ, what can we do to cheer you up?' And I'm like, 'Leave me alone. Don't worry about it.' And I curled ninety-six per cent the next morning." He made his statement on the ice.

But he still had issues. "My point on the whole thing was the rocks were a disaster and you have to understand, you're only going to get one crack at the Olympics. You're representing your country, you've been told you have no chance at the Trials, you win and now you're the favourites to win the gold medal at the Olympic Games, which has never happened. And you get in there knowing that you can perform when the conditions are good, and all of a sudden you have nowhere near the conditions you're used to. And you're supposed to sit back and just enjoy it? I'm not like that. My entire curling career, I've tried to improve curling. I'm very consistent at that. I've changed the rules, I've tried to get sponsorship, I was an icemaker part of my career. It's unacceptable, in my opinion, you could play in the Olympic Games with sub-par conditions. I went to my association and they didn't want to hear anything of it. That was maddening."

CURLING TERMS

PEEL

A takeout shot that removes a rock and rolls out of play itself.

The little assemblage seemed to have lit a spark in the Canadians, who registered a pair of wins the next day over Great Britain and Switzerland. Against Dave Murdoch in the morning, Gushue never trailed en route to a 9-5 decision. It was a little more tense that evening as Canada rallied from a 4-1 deficit after three ends to pull out a 7-5 victory. Ralph Stoeckli stole three in the third end when Gushue's shot clearly picked. The Gushue team maintained that things were, well, just swell. But clearly there were hints of frustration. Following the steal of three, Gushue threw a water bottle to the floor. Later, in the eighth end when Gushue's first shot wrecked on a guard opening up the house for Stoeckli, Howard stepped off the ice, turned his back on his teammates and blurted "Jeezes!"

But there would be no more complaining, at least not publicly, about the ice and rocks. It was a pact that the five curlers had made the night before. "The conditions we had were what we had," said coach McDonald. "You could either choose to bitch and complain about that or choose to deal with the cards you were dealt. This was the situation: these were the rocks and the rocks weren't great. But let's be the best team out there figuring out the rocks. And we decided to bring some fun into it. There would be a two Euro fine if anybody complained about the rocks or the ice. If anybody was prepared to stand up in front of a camera and openly state that they thought the ice was great and the rocks were great, they could earn five Euros back. Nobody lost any money because we didn't have to impose any fines. That's because once we walked out of the meeting, we had it straightened out. By the way, nobody made any money, either."

> ## "This is the most disappointed I've ever been after a win."
> - BRAD GUSHUE

Gushue rebounded after the third end to score five straight points to improve to 3-1 for a three-way tie for first with Murdoch and Lindholm. But he sure didn't sound like someone on top. "This is the most disappointed I've ever been after a win," he said. "It is absolutely the most frustrating time curling out there. It's so difficult to throw good rocks and you have no idea where they're going."

Gushue's next game was against Trulsen, the reigning gold medalist from 2002 and a curler some believed was the best pure shooter in the world. Trulsen did not look like your average curler. Larger than most, Trulsen lumbered around the ice and appeared at times ready to drop the broom and go toe-to-toe with somebody. He also might be the only curler to chew tobacco ... on the ice. Perhaps that's what was causing all those picks.

Gushue got out to a 3-0 lead after two ends, but Trulsen responded with three straight points. Gushue actually tried to seal the game in the fourth end, but lost on the roll of the dice. Holding hammer, Gushue was counting one on his last shot with an opening for a draw to the four foot for two. He elected instead for a trickier angle raise takeout for three, but missed the shot giving Trulsen a steal of one. "That's the way we play. We kind of live by the sword and die by the sword. It didn't work out there," Gushue said. Leading 5-3 through eight ends, Trulsen got his deuce in the ninth end, but Gushue picked up the one point he needed with last shot in the tenth for a 6-5 win.

Gushue had emerged through curling's Olympic ring of fire with nary a blister, sitting in first place with Great Britain at 4-1. While Uusipaavalniemi and, to a lesser degree, Fenson were expected to provide challenges in two of their final four round-robin games, Gushue had dodged some large caliber bullets through five games against the likes of Trulsen, Murdoch, and Stoeckli. "We've played some really tough teams and to be 4-1 in that field, you have to consider yourself lucky," Howard said. But would luck carry them through the second half of the round-robin portion of the schedule? They might have been lucky, but the Gushue team was clearly not firing on all cylinders.

There was still far too much curling left in the round-robin for the Canadians to start chatting about securing a playoff spot, although Gushue did admit he felt he was in a better position than any of the other ten teams. He was sitting comfortably at 4-1. But to some observers there was still something missing, at least when they compared the team to the one that steamrolled through the Trials, losing only once. Why were they still preoccupied with the ice and the rocks? Were Gushue and Howard really getting along? Was the "chemistry" messed up?

If the playoffs were starting the next day, Gushue would be among those curling for a medal. But nobody was taking bets on the likelihood of Canada reaching the gold-medal game. Gushue was curling very well, carrying on from Halifax. But the other key member of the unit, Nichols, was not. In fact, Nichols was near the bottom of the pack among thirds after five games at seventy-three per cent. For Canada to win gold, they needed Mark Nichols at his best.

If there was an upside, it was that the air had been cleared after the Lindholm loss in Game two. It was, says coach McDonald today, a critical time in the Olympic Games for the men's curling team. "No question it could have snowballed into something greater, something that could have wiped out the whole Olympics [for us]," he says. "It was an issue that had to be addressed. But the mark of an excellent team is to be able to sit down and address problems. Nobody is going to go into… the Olympics and not have some problems. You know you're going to have problems. It's how you address them that gives you the opportunity to succeed. And what this team does extremely well is recognize that when issues arise, [you] don't let them fester but sit down and solve them. And that's what we did."

The next challenge for Gushue and his team was Finland. Markku Uusipaavalniemi was a former Finnish champion diver until injury ended that career. So he took up curling, and even constructed his own rink. His other claim to fame was, oddly enough, solving the Rubik's Cube in 25 seconds. Uusipaavalniemi was a talented shooter, a skip who could beat you by himself. And on a Friday afternoon midway through the Winter Olympics, he spelled trouble for Gushue.

The Finn scored three points in the third end and cracked off four more in the seventh in an 8-7 victory, sending Gushue to 4-2 and into a three-way tie for second place with Finland and the surprising United States team. Great Britain remained on top at 5-1 with an 8-2 win over Sweden, virtually eliminating Lindholm from playoff contention at 3-4. The slippery slope for Canada continued on a rainy Saturday in Pinerolo, with a startling 7-6 loss to Italy, dropping Canada to third place and a tie with the home country in the standings. If the air-it-all-out session following the loss to Sweden was a key turning point to Gushue and Co. in Pinerolo, so too was the game against Italy's Joel Retornaz, the rock star wannabe with the designer glasses, tight pants, white shoes, and slicked-back hairdo.

Two different Canadian teams seemed to show up for the Italian game: the first, through five ends, would not have curled with Canada's best junior teams; the second, through the back five and an extra end, gave evidence that Gushue should not be discounted. Canada trailed 5-1 after five ends, as the Palaghiaccio resembled something like a Juventus soccer game with the delirious, flag-waving Italian supporters. Gushue scratched his way back with a deuce in the ninth end and forced the extra end with a steal of one in end ten. With Retornaz holding hammer, Gushue had a pair of rocks in the rings. Retornaz took out Gushue's rock in the eight foot, sticking the shooter, and Gushue, with his final toss, sailed the stone a little too long as it bit the back of the four foot. Undaunted, Retornaz delivered a game-winning shot to the button. "Fantastico!" blurted a Palaghiaccio volunteer. "Bellissimo!"

"For some reason," Gushue said afterwards, "we haven't been getting off to a good start. It's been real bad. We're trying to figure that out and I don't think it's a chemistry thing. We're getting along fine out there. It's just a little bit of misreading the ice and miscalling line and mis-sweeping shots. We're not real sharp the first couple of ends. And this is not the only game this week where it's happened. It's funny, but the first end has been our worst end this week. I don't know how to pinpoint it, but we're going to try and determine that over the next six or seven hours."

Although Retornaz's win thrilled the locals, many of them were probably still trying to figure out this strange bocce-on-ice game. Officially, Italy has more than 500 registered curlers, but there are only about 150 active curlers and only a couple sheets of ice in four cities. If wasn't as if Italy's defeat of Canada was another "Miracle on Ice" like the 1980 Olympics when the U.S. hockey team shocked the Soviet Big Red Machine, but it was still pretty impressive. Heading up Italy's program was a Canadian, Roger Schmidt of Saskatchewan, who curled with Rick Folk in the 1978 Brier. After Turin was awarded the Games, Schmidt was brought in from Switzerland – where he operates a curling academy – to piece together an Italian curling team. "Four years is not a long time to come and beat Canada in the Olympics," he said. "I don't know if the public knows how big this is. They certainly don't know how mammoth the task was." Later that evening, the Canadian Olympic Committee hosted a wine-and-cheese party in honour of both the men's and women's curling teams. The Merlot probably tasted like sour grapes. ●

CHAPTER 11

Russ Howard awoke Sunday morning, February 19, to a chorus of "Happy Birthday" and the usual jabs from his younger teammates. They munched on chocolate cake in honour of Howard's fiftieth birthday, although Gushue quipped that the Hall of Famer barely managed to blow out all the candles. The last flame, joked the skip, flickered a little, but that was the draft from an open window. "He's been throwing paper planes off our balcony with the guys, so he doesn't act fifty, that's for sure."

"Whoever thought you'd come here to play in the Olympics and represent your country at fifty?" beamed Howard. "That would be a pretty cool gift to be asking for." As it happens, Howard was the oldest Canadian Olympian, but he wasn't the oldest curler in Pinerolo. New Zealand lead Lorne DePape was also fifty, but had Howard beat by ten months. And the two were whippersnappers compared to American fifth Scott Baird, who was fifty-four.

Fortunately, the good cheer continued on to the ice against New Zealand as Canada romped to a 9-1, seven-end win. The mood was much darker back in Turin after the Canadian men's hockey team was shut out 2-0 for the second consecutive game. The loss to Finland followed a shocking 2-0 setback to Switzerland on Saturday. Meanwhile, on the curling ice, Gushue was 5-3 and lodged in the fourth and final playoff spot. The United States, Finland, and Great Britain were assured of a playoff spot, while Canada needed a win over Pete Fenson's United States team in their final round-robin game on Monday to advance to the medal round and avoid a dreaded tiebreaker.

Before the biggest game of the tournament, if not of his life, Jamie Korab woke up feeling a little squeamish. And it only got worse. "He's got an explosive lower body injury," quipped Mike Adam of his teammate. With Korab back in residence suffering from stomach flu, Adam was inserted into the lineup at lead in the pivotal game against Fenson, the pizza maker from Bemidji, Minnesota, just 150 kilometers from the Canadian border. Luckily for Adam, he got a couple of ends in against New Zealand to work out any Olympic butterflies. He had been throwing rocks all week, but only in practice. "Yeah," he laughed, "just me and the janitor."

With Adam curling eighty-three per cent, the Canadians didn't miss a beat. Trailing 3-2 after seven ends, Gushue picked up a deuce in the eighth end and stole points in the ninth and 10th for a 6-3 decision over the United States, vaulting them into the playoffs and setting the stage for another rematch against Fenson in Wednesday's semifinals. Once again, the post-game talk centered as much on the ice conditions as it did on Canada's semifinal berth. But as McDonald had suggested, Canada focused its attention on trying to get a handle on the ice conditions rather than whining about them.

"It's starting to get a little like a guessing game," Gushue said. "The further you go out [on the side of the sheet], the more you curl. There's about eighty different ways to get to the button. It's tough, but the team that gets a little better read on it is going to win ninety per cent of the time. That's what it's come down to. So you have to be prepared before the game. And there's no one we'd rather have keeping an eye to it than Russ. I think he's the best in the world. And myself and Mark are also good, so we have three good eyes who can read the ice and hopefully get the broom to the right spot."

The celebration started after Canada defeated Finland for the Olympic men's curling gold medal. Mark Nichols, right, established himself as one of the world's elite curlers with a pair of magnificent games in the semifinal and gold-medal games. *(Canadian Press photo)*

With the win, Canada finished second at 6-3. The United States and Great Britain were also 6-3, but Gushue beat both in the round-robin. Finland finished on top at 7-2.

"We've made the playoffs here, made the final four, knocked off the defending champions [Norway]," said Howard. "We can only do so much in one week. I'm proud of the guys one way or another."

Lost in all the talk about ice and rocks and speculation that the Gushue-Howard marriage was souring was the play of Nichols. It was, simply, not good. Not that Nichols was costing Gushue games. But he wasn't winning many, either. The final round-robin stats showed Nichols curling seventy-seven per cent, fifth among thirds. Of course, curling stats, more than any other numbers in sport, can be subjective. The truth was that Nichols wasn't, well, Nichols. And while no one said it, this was a major concern.

Then, in a game that would determine if Canada played for gold, silver, bronze, or fourth place, Nichols stepped to the plate and in baseball lingo "hit for the cycle." He curled a sizzling ninety-four per cent, setting Gushue up to do his thing with last shot as Canada marched to an 11-5 pasting over Pizza Pete in the semifinal on Wednesday at Pinerolo. Silver, at least, was theirs. "By far, that was the best game we've played," gushed Gushue. "I could tell from the first end we were back. And I attribute that to Mark Nichols."

Canada led 4-3 after five ends and was clinging to a 6-5 lead when the Americans threw it down the toilet in the ninth end. After third Shawn Rojeski blew a couple of shots, including one hog line violation (when he failed to release the stone at the hog line, or the line where the thrower must let go of the rock during delivery), Canada took control and set up three stones at the top of the house. Fenson was light on his last shot and Gushue made an easy peel to score five and draw handshakes from the United States team. Then, on the night before their semifinal game, the Canadian men's curling team watched Canada's women's hockey team dismantle Sweden 4-1 to win the gold medal. Nichols said it was a special moment: watching the hockey players receive their gold medals and hearing the Canadian anthem played. The curlers, he said, were deeply inspired.

Whatever conjured the magic, it worked on Nichols. That, and a little bit of extra practice. On the day before the date with the United States, Canada retreated to the Palaghiaccio's practice facility and Nichols delivered a couple of runback shots. As Howard and Gushue looked on, Nichols was asked what he felt he was doing differently from the Halifax

Trials. Because of the unpredictable ice, the third said, he was easing up on his push out of the hack. All three agreed it was time for Nichols to stop over-thinking shots and revert back to doing what he does best. Nichols, Gushue said, made about eight straight runbacks, all right on the money. "You could see the sparkle in his eye," Gushue said. "He's the key to this team. He had it out there today and when he's shooting like that, we're going to win a heck of a lot of games."

The win against the United States set up a gold medal meeting between Gushue and Uusipaavalniemi, who had dispatched Murdoch 4-3. Gushue was 1-1 lifetime against the Finns, their win coming at The National Grand Slam event in Port Hawesbury, Nova Scotia. "They're a little bit easier to read than the Americans," Gushue said. "Each time we've played, we've gotten different games out of them [the Americans]. With Markku, you know they set up the games around him. A lot of the strategy is him making the big shots, and if he makes them, they're tough to beat. If he's not making them, you can crack some big ends on them." Gushue's words would prove to be more prophetic than he could ever have imagined.

> "By far, that was the best game we've played. I could tell from the first end we were back. And I attribute that to Mark Nichols."
>
> - BRAD GUSHUE

Meanwhile, the curlers didn't know it at the time, but they were making big headlines back home. In fact, they were the lead item on most sportscasts across the country. And nowhere was the news bigger than in Newfoundland and Labrador. Premier Danny Williams ordered the province's schools to close early on Friday, February 24, so the students and teachers could all watch the game. Offices across the province were effectively shut down as workers lugged in television sets and ordered pizzas, hoping to witness something special unfold. For an entire province, the Olympic men's gold medal curling game was going to be their Paul Henderson moment. Newfoundlanders and Labradorians were all going to be able to recall where they were on February 24, 2006.

In and around the city of St. John's, traffic was noticeably light and the city was eerily quiet. Men and women, young and old, those who followed curling and those who didn't have a clue about the game – they were all tuned in to the CBC. In Mount Pearl, a St. John's suburb where Gushue grew up, O'Donel High School was planning a party for 700. Gushue's old school was showing the game live on the big screen. "[O'Donel] Patriots: Look at us now!" read one school banner.

Inside the St. John's Curling Club, hundreds more filled the building, many dressed in red and white. Memorial University, which counted Gushue and Nichols as its alumni, was also setting up a big screen in its Field House. Even Premier Williams, who was in Ottawa for the first ministers meetings, took advantage of a break to watch the match – right after he made a pre-game phone call to Gushue.

Ironically, most of the country's best curlers were in St. John's to play in the Masters of Curling at Mile One Stadium. Gushue, of course, was supposed to be the main attraction for the Masters, which ended up a box office nightmare. Most curling fans had understandably opted to stay home and watch Gushue on television rather than see Kevin Martin, Randy Ferbey, Glenn Howard, and Jeff Stoughton live at Mile One. And in a classic case of Murphy's Law, the city was hit with the harshest storm of the season on Friday night. The blast of winter shut down St. John's on Saturday and left everyone still digging out on Sunday. Masters local organizer Garry Stamp later joked it was only him, the rink attendants, and the curlers who were at Mile One over the weekend.

Just as he had predicted prior to the Olympics, Kevin Martin maintained that Gushue would beat the Finnish "alphabet" in the final, even though Uusipaavalniemi had gotten the upper hand on Gushue in the round-robin. "They will win," Martin told St. John's reporters at the Masters. "I had them winning the semis by five and the final by five, and they won the semi by six. If they play like they did in their games against the United States, Finland can't win. They're not at that level."

The quaint Palaghiaccio was filled to near capacity, many of them donning red and white for the occasion, and Canada's press corps was certainly out in full strength. Sitting nervously at one end of the rink was Ray Gushue, wearing his now-familiar "Brad's Dad!" shirt. If Brad longed to have Maureen Gushue in Italy, so too did her husband. Ray Gushue probably had a few more

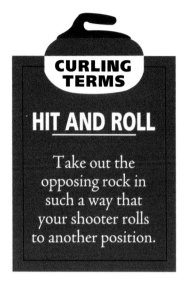

CURLING TERMS

HIT AND ROLL

Take out the opposing rock in such a way that your shooter rolls to another position.

dancing butterflies than usual after the first end when the Finns grabbed a 2-0 lead with last rock. While Canada had been gaining momentum with four straight wins, Finland had been on quite a roll itself, reeling off six consecutive victories. Now they were off to a good start in the only game that really mattered.

Gushue rebounded with a deuce of his own in the second end and stole points in the third and fourth ends before Uusipaavalniemi counted one in the fifth following a measurement. While Canada led by only one point at the break, it was the Gushue foursome that seemed to have a firm grip on the game. Just as Martin had forecast, Finland was really no match for Canada. More to the point, it was no match for Nichols. His display of curling in the 2006 Olympic final was arguably the finest individual effort of any curler in an event of this magnitude. Nichols curled an out-of-this-world ninety-seven per cent in the game.

It was Nichols who set up the fateful sixth end with perhaps the finest shot in the Olympic tournament. With his last shot, Nichols executed a perfect long raise double takeout, a high-risk toss that saw the Canadian stone hit a Finnish centerline guard about eight feet outside the twelve-foot, which in turn bumped out a second Finnish guard just outside the twelve-foot and a third Finnish stone resting on the four-foot. The last ousted rock just shaved a Canadian stone sitting on the button as Gushue counted three.

Uusipaavalniemi wrecked on guards on both his shots as Gushue, with last shot, stared incredulously at six yellow rocks counting. "My heart started absolutely pounding," he said. "I looked around and did the math. We're one up and we get six and now we're seven up and there's no way we're losing."

Back in Newfoundland and Labrador, it was sheer pandemonium. Cheers of "Here we go Canada, Here we go!" echoed throughout the province. Some sang the province's unofficial anthem, the "Ode to Newfoundland." Friends and strangers alike celebrated and embraced. The victory party started early and there was no telling when it would end. It was "Henderson ... has scored for Canada" all over again. This time magnified by ten in Canada's youngest province. And in Southlands, at No. 15 Jacaranda Place, a proud mother cried.

Back inside the Palaghiaccio, the scene was a little more surreal. For what seemed like several seconds, the rink fell silent, as if the fans were trying to understand if what they were seeing was real or a mirage. As Gushue slid down the ice for the last shot of the sixth end, a mounting buzz swept through the building. Then he was heavy on his draw for seven (when was the last time you heard that at the Olympics?). There would be no conversion on the touchdown.

Maureen Gushue couldn't travel to Italy because she was undergoing chemotherapy, but her son was in constant contact throughout the two weeks of the Games. One of the Olympics' most endearing moments was when he called her immediately after winning gold. *(Canadian Press photo)*

For the next twenty minutes, the teams played the final two ends, but they were a mere formality. "It was kind of a deflating moment when we got the six, to be honest," said Howard. "You expected all along to be one up and Brad has to make a raise to win, or two up or something. And instead, 'Well, we won, but now what do we do?' They were obviously deflated and we were [wondering], 'What now?' [When] Brad's rock slides right through for the seven, were we supposed to be happy or sad?"

They finally shook hands after eight ends as Canada won its twentieth medal – and its sixth gold – of the Turin Winter Olympic Games. Gushue turned to Howard. This was the curler he had looked up to, the legend who had guided the youngsters across the bumpy ice of the Olympic Trials, and the man who had been at the centre of a quasi controversy earlier in the Games. The two men hugged. And then, in one of the signature moments of the Games, Gushue caught his cell phone tossed to him by Mike Adam and hit the speed dial. "Mom, we did it," he said, after imploring her through a CBC camera crew to answer the phone. "I hope you're feeling good." He was aching for her to be there, and relieved when she picked up the phone. He'd had a busy signal on the first try, prompting his on-air plea.

"Over the last couple of days of the Olympics," said his sister, Natasha, who was home with her mother, "we'd had lots and lots of calls from people wanting to wish Brad and the team luck and offering prayers for Mom. After the final, there was an eighty-year-old woman from Gambo [in central Newfoundland] who had called just before Brad tried to reach us. God bless her, but we couldn't get her off the phone in time."

The conversation with his mother did not last long. Gushue was whisked away for a live television interview, and by this time a flood of emotions built up over the past two weeks and more came pouring out. On national television, Gushue broke down. Truth is, there weren't many dry eyes in Newfoundland and Labrador, or anywhere in Canada.

"I didn't get much in because she was crying, and that caused me to cry," he said. "I haven't cried like that in a while. Hopefully, people won't call me too much of a 'sook' when I get home. I've thought about her every hour of every day since I've been here. This morning was tough for me, a very emotional morning because I knew that win or lose, I wanted her here. But she's happy, and nobody better get in my way when we get home to the airport because she's the first one I want to see."

While the storyline of the day was Gushue and his Mom, with Howard a close second, almost lost in the hoopla was Mark Nichols – which seemed fitting for the subdued vice-skip. Not that he was overlooked by his teammates. "This is a game that puts him on the map," Korab said of Nichols. "The level we're competing at? I've seen him play a better Super League game at our own club. But to play it at the Olympic Games with millions and millions of people watching at home? Come on."

"The beginning of the week," said Nichols, "I was just saying, 'Hang in there, guys. I'll start making shots.' I was lucky to do it in the two biggest games of our lives."

As the celebration continued, the hugs and high-fives seemingly never-ending, Howard was holding court with the media. Always quotable Howard, and able to play the media as good as anyone, he is a reporter's best friend. He recalled his wonderful ride that started with a phone call in April of 2005. He remembered what the skeptics had said, that it wouldn't work, that Howard was too old to curl with twenty-somethings. We were just five guys, he said, five curlers with a purpose. Outside the playful old guy jokes, he was just one of the boys. "And we know what happens behind the scenes," says Gushue. "We live in the same room at night. You can't look at a guy as a legend when he snores and leaves his clothes all over the place."

If there had been any acrimony early in the Olympics, it was now forgotten. All that talk of bad ice and lousy rocks, all the complaining and whining and infighting, had been swept away. All that mattered now was gold.

AFTERWORD

Life has not, and never will be, quite the same for Brad Gushue, Mark Nichols, Russ Howard, Jamie Korab, Mike Adam, and Toby McDonald. That message hit home when they arrived in Canada to a huge reception from fans at Toronto's Pearson International Airport. But it was nothing compared to the welcome that awaited them in St. John's. Even arriving in the wee hours of a Tuesday morning, over 1,000 fans burst into applause as the six made their way down the escalator in the arrivals terminal. Some fans drove more than an hour into St. John's just to be part of the historic moment.

"I was here in December when they won the Trials," said Jeff Thomas, their first coach, "and you recognized all the curling faces. Tonight, I don't recognize anybody. That's how big this is. These are not curlers here. These are people who are happy to be wrapped up in the moment."

A family portrait: Brad Gushue, Maureen Gushue, Ray Gushue and little Parker, Brad's nephew, upon the team's return from Turin. *(Don Power/The Express photo)*

At one point, Nichols said, he took a pee break and a dozen people followed him into the bathroom.

The team arrived wearing their Canada red and white outfits, and, of course, their beautiful gold awards. Korab had a matching ensemble going, with a brand new pair of white leather Italian loafers. They all signed autographs, posed for pictures, and recalled for the benefit of fans and the media many of the final moments of the final game.

"Willie [Finnish third Willie Makela] walked right towards me and shook my hand," Korab said. "It was such a sign of relief. 'Oh my God, we actually did it.' Then the realization really hit when we all got together and hugged. 'We're Olympic gold medalists!'"

After the final in Pinerolo, McDonald said the Gushue victory would be recalled in Canada fifty years from now, and another 250 years in Newfoundland and Labrador. Clearly there will be lots of reminders. The City of St. John's has named six streets after the team, all in Southlands, and Gushue and Krista Tibbo, who married in September, may build a house on Brad Gushue Crescent. A newly-constructed major thoroughfare in the city has been christened Team Gushue Highway. The Town of Harbour Grace has named one of its streets Jamie's Way. In Mount Pearl, where Gushue grew up, one of its sports arenas is now named Team Gushue Sportsplex. And Memorial University has given all six of the Olympic heroes an honorary Doctorate. "You always dream of winning Olympic gold," says Nichols, "but you never wake up and think to have a street named after you. That stuff is cool, all the stuff that comes with it. We're recognized quite a bit. You go to a McDonald's and you hear whispers and you see elbows nudge."

Shortly after arriving home, the team was invited to Regina, Saskatchewan for the Tim Hortons Brier where the public love affair continued. Thousands of curling fans showed up at the Brier Patch for a question-and-answer session with the curlers. One female fan asked Gushue if he'd marry her, move to Saskatchewan, and curl for that province. Some female fans even asked the curler to autograph certain parts of their upper anatomy. "I've been asked that a lot," Gushue says sheepishly. Meanwhile, Korab had an amusing visit to Eston, Saskatchewan, population about 1,000. "I went to bingo and the older ladies were really happy to see me," he told the Edmonton Sun. "Then I won eighty dollars and they booed me."

Gushue's gold-medal victory, with his mother home receiving chemotherapy treatments, was the feel-good story of the Olympics. But there was no doubt the Canadian darling of the Turin Games was Winnipeg's Cindy Klassen and her record five medals: one gold, two silver, and two bronze. Her popularity is evident on the sponsorship front. After the Olympic flame was extinguished, sponsors were positively giddy over the prospects of signing the personable athlete with her Mennonite wholesomeness. Klassen has now set new standards for endorsements by a Canadian amateur athlete. She received a big deal from MTS, the Manitoba telecommunications company, and she has renegotiated a multi-year deal with McDonald's. She is also sponsored by Oakley, maker of the popular eyewear.

Her agent, Toronto's Elliott Kerr, who also represents the Gushue curlers, claims the deals are worth more than a million dollars each over the life of the agreements. "There's a focus on Olympic sport in Canada like there's never been before," opined David Bedford, executive director of revenue, brand management, and communications for the Canadian Olympic Committee, to the National Post. "The investments by Canadian companies are what they've never been before."

Unfortunately, that flow of money has not reached the curlers in Newfoundland. They have certainly been busy since the Games. Gushue travelled virtually every weekend making appearances. One of those was at the Juno Awards in Halifax. But when it came to talking turkey and negotiating big sponsorship deals, there were not as many opportunities as the curlers had imagined.

"We had more television exposure than any other sport in the whole Olympics," Howard said. "The baby boomer generation is watching and yet there hasn't been a huge interest in us. It boggles the mind." Similarly, there weren't many job offers for Gushue and Nichols, both of whom are intelligent, well-spoken university graduates. But this comes as no surprise to Gerry Peckham of the Canadian Curling Association. He acknowledges with regret that, despite the autographing invitations, curling just isn't sexy enough. "I appreciate it that it's a gold medal, but his [Gushue's] opportunities are predominantly going to be in Newfoundland," Peckham said. "The [Sandra] Schmirler team did nothing really with their gold medal [in 1998], and she was already a household name. What it's an indication of, in my opinion, is the fact that corporate Canada hasn't bought into or aligned itself with Canadian amateur athletes. There's not an awful lot of money that moves from corporate Canada directly into an athlete's pockets, let alone the programs and services that support them," offers Peckham.

In the few short months since Torino, the Gushue team has undergone more change. McDonald has stepped aside as coach, and Howard will only be curling with the team in specialty events. He will curl with his son in New Brunswick in the hopes of reaching the Brier. While Adam seemed the logical choice to replace Howard, the Gushue team has dipped into Alberta where Chris Schille has been recruited to curl second stone. Adam will remain as fifth man.

As for the dearth of sponsorship and other business opportunities, Gushue and his fellow curlers have made up for it elsewhere. They are all revered in their home province, as is Howard in New Brunswick, and they are heroes to their fans across Canada. They are considered sports idols by children, particularly in Newfoundland and Labrador. They will be

Canada's first men's Olympic curling gold medal came at the 2006
Turin Winter Games and it was won by the Brad Gushue curling team
from Newfoundland and Labrador. Showing their gold jewelry are,
from left, Brad Gushue, Mark Nichols, Russ Howard, Jamie Korab and
Mike Adam. Missing from photo is coach Toby McDonald.
(Canadian Press photo)

responsible for an unprecedented growth and interest in curling. And they
have won something that no other male curler has achieved in the history
of the game in Canada – an Olympic gold medal.

"We're the first men [in Canadian curling] to win a gold medal,"
Gushue says proudly. "And 100 years from now, people are still going to
say we're the first team.

I'm sure there will be more, but there will always be the first one. This
is very special."

ACKNOWLEDGEMENTS

On the 26th day of February, 2006, just as the curtains were closing on the 20th edition of the Winter Olympic Games, a number of journalists gathered in a quaint little pizzeria and pub near our temporary apartments in Grugliasco, just outside Turin, Italy. Red wine flowed freely as my Globe and Mail friends and I toasted the Games into the wee hours of the morning. For Roy MacGregor and Christie Blatchford, flying halfway around the world to cover a major Canadian news story was not such a big deal. For me, it was very different. This was my first Olympics, and the Brad Gushue curling team – the heroes of my story – had emerged with the gold medal.

I recall MacGregor asking if I had considered a book on the Gushue team. I hadn't, of course. He suggested I give it a whirl, and Rock Stars was born. But not without a lot of sweat. To write a news story or column is one thing. To pen a book is a different matter. Thanks to MacGregor's encouragement and guidance (from the Wayne Gretzky of sportswriting no less), you are holding the finished product. To Roy, I offer my sincere appreciation. A big thank-you also goes out to all my friends at The Globe, especially the incomparable Blatchford, and the very talented Dave Naylor.

There are many people to thank for this project. At the top of the list are my bosses: The Telegram's publisher, Miller Ayre, and editor Russell Wangersky, who both knew a great story when they saw it. They sent me to Halifax for the Olympic Trials and then sprung for the big expenses of the Turin Games. My gratitude also goes out to Creative Book Publishing, and especially Keith Soper, Donna Francis, Kerri Cull, and my editor Don Sedgwick. Thanks also to Scott Courage for providing me with a place to write, away from home where a four-year-old fought to go to bed each night.

An enormous thank-you goes out to Brad Gushue, Mark Nichols, Russ Howard, Jamie Korab, Mike Adam, and Toby McDonald. Together they created a marvelous story, and I am proud and honoured to say I was there to witness every minute of it.

Finally, a very special thank-you goes to Kimberly Short and Cameron Short. My family coped without complaint when I was often away from home covering curling events, even as our town was lashed by winter storms. Kim's words of encouragement in particular helped me through some moments of anxiety and self-doubt. This project would not have been possible without their love and support.

Robin Short
St. John's, NL
July, 2006

Robin Short was born in St. John's, Newfoundland and has spent all forty-one of his years in the city. Sports Editor of *The Telegram*, the province's largest daily newspaper, Robin discovered the newspaper business in 1985 when he was hired at the ripe age of twenty. In addition to his work at *The Telegram*, he is a contributor to *The Hockey News* and has written for the *National Post*, and a number of other newspapers and publications, including *Leafs Nation*. Throughout his sports-reporting career, Robin has covered a number of events including Canada's 1985 World Cup of Soccer qualifying game, seven Canada Summer and Winter Games, three NHL Entry Drafts, the 2005 Canadian Olympic Curling Trials, and the XX Winter Olympic Games. Robin is a 2003 winner of the Atlantic Journalism Award for sports reporting and was a finalist for the 2005 award. In 1996, Robin's column, 'What Hockey's All About', was published in Trent Frayne's *All-Stars: An Anthology of Canada's Best Sportswriting*. Robin and his wife, Kimberly, are the proud parents of a son, Cameron.